OPPOSING VIEWPOINTS® SERIES

I0812913

Ethics in Politics

Other Books of Related Interest

Opposing Viewpoints Series

America's Great Divide
Government Gridlock
The Politics of Climate

At Issue Series

Is America a Democracy or an Oligarchy?
Partisanship
The Politicization of the Supreme Court

Current Controversies Series

The Capitol Riot: Fragile Democracy
Media Trustworthiness
The Politics and Science of COVID-19

> "Congress shall make no law … abridging the freedom of speech, or of the press."
>
> *First Amendment to the U.S. Constitution*

The basic foundation of our democracy is the First Amendment guarantee of freedom of expression. The Opposing Viewpoints series is dedicated to the concept of this basic freedom and the idea that it is more important to practice it than to enshrine it.

OPPOSING VIEWPOINTS® SERIES

Ethics in Politics

Gary Wiener, Book Editor

GREENHAVEN PUBLISHING

Published in 2024 by Greenhaven Publishing, LLC
2544 Clinton Street,
Buffalo NY 14224

Copyright © 2024 by Greenhaven Publishing, LLC

First Edition

All rights reserved. No part of this book may be reproduced in any form without permission in writing from the publisher, except by a reviewer.

Articles in Greenhaven Publishing anthologies are often edited for length to meet page requirements. In addition, original titles of these works are changed to clearly present the main thesis and to explicitly indicate the author's opinion. Every effort is made to ensure that Greenhaven Publishing accurately reflects the original intent of the authors. Every effort has been made to trace the owners of the copyrighted material.

Cover image: Marian Weyo/Shutterstock.com and metamorworks/Shutterstock.com

Library of Congress CataloginginPublication Data
Names: Wiener, Gary, editor.
Title: Ethics in politics / edited by Gary Wiener.
Description: First edition. | New York : Greenhaven Publishing, 2024. | Series: Opposing viewpoints | Includes bibliographic references and index.
Identifiers: ISBN 9781534509573 (pbk.) | ISBN 9781534509580 (library bound)
Subjects: LCSH: United States--Politics and government--Juvenile literature. | Political corruption--United States--Juvenile literature. | Political culture--United States--Juvenile literature.
Classification: LCC JK2249.E844 2024 | DDC 324.273--dc23

Manufactured in the United States of America

Website: http://greenhavenpublishing.com

Contents

Chapter 3: Has Dishonesty from Politicians Gone Too Far?

Chapter 4: Is Political Lobbying an Ethical System?

The Importance of Opposing Viewpoints

Perhaps every generation experiences a period in time in which the populace seems especially polarized, starkly divided on the important issues of the day and gravitating toward the far ends of the political spectrum and away from a consensus-facilitating middle ground. The world that today's students are growing up in and that they will soon enter into as active and engaged citizens is deeply fragmented in just this way. Issues relating to terrorism, immigration, women's rights, minority rights, race relations, health care, taxation, wealth and poverty, the environment, policing, military intervention, the proper role of government—in some ways, perennial issues that are freshly and uniquely urgent and vital with each new generation—are currently roiling the world.

If we are to foster a knowledgeable, responsible, active, and engaged citizenry among today's youth, we must provide them with the intellectual, interpretive, and critical-thinking tools and experience necessary to make sense of the world around them and of the all-important debates and arguments that inform it. After all, the outcome of these debates will in large measure determine the future course, prospects, and outcomes of the world and its peoples, particularly its youth. If they are to become successful members of society and productive and informed citizens, students need to learn how to evaluate the strengths and weaknesses of someone else's arguments, how to sift fact from opinion and fallacy, and how to test the relative merits and validity of their own opinions against the known facts and the best possible available information. The landmark series Opposing Viewpoints has been providing students with just such critical-thinking skills and exposure to the debates surrounding society's most urgent contemporary issues for many years, and it continues to serve this essential role with undiminished commitment, care, and rigor.

The key to the series's success in achieving its goal of sharpening students' critical-thinking and analytic skills resides in its title—

Opposing Viewpoints. In every intriguing, compelling, and engaging volume of this series, readers are presented with the widest possible spectrum of distinct viewpoints, expert opinions, and informed argumentation and commentary, supplied by some of today's leading academics, thinkers, analysts, politicians, policy makers, economists, activists, change agents, and advocates. Every opinion and argument anthologized here is presented objectively and accorded respect. There is no editorializing in any introductory text or in the arrangement and order of the pieces. No piece is included as a "straw man," an easy ideological target for cheap point-scoring. As wide and inclusive a range of viewpoints as possible is offered, with no privileging of one particular political ideology or cultural perspective over another. It is left to each individual reader to evaluate the relative merits of each argument—as he or she sees it, and with the use of ever-growing critical-thinking skills—and grapple with his or her own assumptions, beliefs, and perspectives to determine how convincing or successful any given argument is and how the reader's own stance on the issue may be modified or altered in response to it.

This process is facilitated and supported by volume, chapter, and selection introductions that provide readers with the essential context they need to begin engaging with the spotlighted issues, with the debates surrounding them, and with their own perhaps shifting or nascent opinions on them. In addition, guided reading and discussion questions encourage readers to determine the authors' point of view and purpose, interrogate and analyze the various arguments and their rhetoric and structure, evaluate the arguments' strengths and weaknesses, test their claims against available facts and evidence, judge the validity of the reasoning, and bring into clearer, sharper focus the reader's own beliefs and conclusions and how they may differ from or align with those in the collection or those of their classmates.

Research has shown that reading comprehension skills improve dramatically when students are provided with compelling, intriguing, and relevant "discussable" texts. The subject matter of these collections could not be more compelling, intriguing, or urgently relevant to today's students and the world they are poised to inherit. The anthologized articles and the reading and discussion questions that are included with them also provide the basis for stimulating, lively, and passionate classroom debates. Students who are compelled to anticipate objections to their own argument and identify the flaws in those of an opponent read more carefully, think more critically, and steep themselves in relevant context, facts, and information more thoroughly. In short, using discussable text of the kind provided by every single volume in the Opposing Viewpoints series encourages close reading, facilitates reading comprehension, fosters research, strengthens critical thinking, and greatly enlivens and energizes classroom discussion and participation. The entire learning process is deepened, extended, and strengthened.

For all of these reasons, Opposing Viewpoints continues to be exactly the right resource at exactly the right time—when we most need to provide readers with the critical-thinking tools and skills that will not only serve them well in school but also in their careers and their daily lives as decision-making family members, community members, and citizens. This series encourages respectful engagement with and analysis of opposing viewpoints and fosters a resulting increase in the strength and rigor of one's own opinions and stances. As such, it helps make readers "future ready," and that readiness will pay rich dividends for the readers themselves, for the citizenry, for our society, and for the world at large.

Introduction

> *"We hang the petty thieves and appoint the great ones to public office."*
>
> *—Aesop, Greek storyteller*

Ethics in politics: the very phrase may be considered oxymoronic by many observers of political life. As writer Arthur Koestler has said, "The principle that the end justifies the means is and remains the only rule of political ethics; anything else is just a vague chatter and melts away between one's fingers." Mark Twain was even harsher in his famous jab at America's legislative body: "There is no distinctly native American criminal class except Congress," the humorist wrote. Nobel Laureate Bob Dylan summed up the state of ethics in politics quite simply when he wrote: "Morality has nothing to do with politics."

These scathing observations don't seem like exaggeration given the divisiveness and political attacks that are associated with the current political climate. As for Twain's remark about Congress being a criminal class, New York Republican Congressman George Santos and New Jersey Democratic Senator Bob Menendez both serve as real life examples of Twain's satiric wisdom. Congressman Santos allegedly conned his way into the House of Representatives through false statements and fraudulent fundraising. In May of 2023, Santos was indicted on 13 counts of federal fraud and money laundering charges. In September of the same year, Senator Menendez and his wife were charged in an indictment claiming that Menendez allegedly accepted luxury goods and substantial monetary bribes in exchange for performing corrupt acts, including providing sensitive information to the Egyptian government.

These two high profile corruption cases pale in comparison to the charges leveled against the former President of the United States, Donald J. Trump. Between 2022 and 2023 four separate criminal cases and two additional civil cases have involved the erstwhile president, who continued to campaign for the 2024 presidential election in between surrendering to authorities in New York City, Washington, DC, and Atlanta to face criminal charges. In four separate cases, Trump has been accused of attempting to overturn the 2020 election and inciting the January 6th riot at the Capitol in Washington, DC; willfully retaining highly classified national defense information and conspiring to obstruct justice; interfering in Georgia's presidential election of 2020; and falsifying business records in the Stormy Daniels hush money scheme.

Trump was subsequently arrested and booked. In the Georgia case, he showed up at Atlanta's Fulton County jail, where authorities later released a mug shot, a first for a U.S. president. Strangely, though, Trump was not the first president arrested for crimes. In 1872, while occupying the White House, Ulysses S. Grant was detained by a police officer, William Henry West, for speeding in his horse and buggy on the streets of Washington, DC. His offense, though dangerous, did not rise to the level of that of other subsequent presidents who were never indicted for crimes. He ended up paying $20 (about $500 in today's money).

One hundred years later in 1972, a much more historically prominent crime occurred when Richard M. Nixon and his staff attempted to cover up a break-in at the Watergate Hotel, where a group of Republican operatives had stolen sensitive documents and installed wiretaps in the office of the Democratic National Committee (DNC). Forty federal officials were indicted and found guilty of various crimes. Nixon himself was named as an "unindicted co-conspirator" solely because no one was sure if a sitting president could be indicted. That precedent had ramifications in the twenty-first century when President Trump was similarly named as an unindicted co-conspirator in the Stormy Daniels case.

In 2018, the National Archive released a document showing that Nixon would have been indicted for bribery, conspiracy, obstruction of justice, and obstruction of a criminal investigation. After threats of impeachment, Nixon resigned from office in 1973 and was replaced by his vice president, Gerald R. Ford. With charges against Nixon still looming, in September 1974 Ford issued a blanket pardon absolving his predecessor of all crimes. "Our long national nightmare is over," he famously pronounced, but his declaration was premature. Questionable presidential ethics have marred the tenure of almost all of Nixon's successors.

The public was not happy about the pardon. Ford's approval rating plummeted and he lost his re-election bid in 1976. Presidential historians have noted that letting Nixon get away with his crimes has led to subsequent presidents acting unethically, even illegally. Some point to a direct line between Presidents Nixon and Trump. "If Ford, 49 years ago, had performed his duty to the country and the Constitution, Trump would just be another ex-president who went off the rails—not the far-and-away frontrunner for the 2024 GOP nomination," wrote political journalist Eleanor Clift.[1] Instead, because Nixon was never prosecuted, Trump was able to seize on his predecessor's words as justification for his actions: "...when the President does it, that means that it is not illegal."

After Nixon, the next president to flirt with impeachment charges and possible indictment was Bill Clinton. Clinton had been mired in an inappropriate relationship with a White House intern named Monica Lewinsky. A special prosecutor, Kenneth Starr, had been looking into a previous sexual harassment lawsuit involving a woman named Paula Jones when the Lewinsky affair came to light. Under oath, Clinton, trying to save his presidency, lied about the Lewinsky affair. He was subsequently impeached for perjury and obstruction of justice, but acquitted in a Senate trial. Nevertheless, criminal charges against Clinton were still looming as he was set to leave office in 2001. Clinton struck a last minute deal with prosecutors that put an end to his legal woes. As reported in the *Washington Post*, "With just hours left in office, President

Clinton reached a deal with the independent counsel yesterday that ensures he will avoid indictment for his misleading statements about Lewinsky. In exchange, Clinton offered prosecutor Robert W. Ray something he had never before been willing to give: a forthright admission that he gave false testimony under oath."[2]

One could certainly say that Clinton's impeachment and the criminal charges were politically motivated, but one could also accurately assert that Trump's were as well. Republicans would never have dared to impeach or try Donald Trump. The dirty work was left to congressional Democrats. On the other hand, Nixon finally resigned when a group of his fellow Republicans told him they could no longer support him. Times have changed. Political ethics have become murkier, and doing the right thing seems like a quaint old tradition.

Opposing Viewpoints: Ethics in Politics presents a wide range of opinions that debate and clarify the nature of political morality. Conservative as well as progressive views on ethics in politics are presented, along with those in between. Many viewpoints included within offer possible solutions to ethical quandaries in government.

Notes

1. Eleanor Clift. "Gerald Ford's Pardon of Nixon Is Why Donald Trump Can Still Run for President," *Daily Beast,* August 8, 2023, https://www.thedailybeast.com/gerald-fords-pardon-of-nixon-is-why-donald-trump-can-still-run-for-president.
2. John F. Harris and Bill Miller. "In a Deal, Clinton Avoids Indictment," *Washington Post*, January 20, 2001, https://www.washingtonpost.com/archive/politics/2001/01/20/in-a-deal-clinton-avoids-indictment/bb80cc4c-e72c-40c1-bb72-55b2b81c3065/.

OPPOSING VIEWPOINTS® SERIES

Chapter 1

Does *Citizens United* Encourage Unethical Political Donations?

Chapter Preface

The Supreme Court's *Citizens United* decision validated the concept that corporations could be treated as individual people in the United States. The *Citizens United* case involved campaign finance laws, which had been previously tightened in an attempt to bring transparency to political donations. As Supreme Court Justice Louis Brandeis stated over a century ago: "Sunlight is said to be the best of disinfectants." When it comes to political donations, hiding their source is often seen to be shady, and the custom promotes abuse. Yet, in the *Citizens United* decision, the Supreme Court lent its imprimatur to the practice.

The case is named for Citizens United, a conservative non-profit organization that attempted to broadcast a film critical of Democratic presidential candidate Hillary Clinton in the run-up to the 2008 Democratic primary elections. The broadcast would have violated the 2002 Bipartisan Campaign Reform Act, which prevented a labor union or corporation from making an "electioneering communication" within 30 days of a primary or 60 days of an election, or making any expenditure supporting or rejecting an individual candidate at any time. The case, known as *Citizens United v. Federal Election Commission*, went through the lower courts. Then, in a high-profile Supreme Court ruling in 2010, the justices ruled, essentially along "party" lines (five conservative justices versus four liberal ones), that corporations were granted First Amendment rights. The decision meant that corporate political spending was protected speech under the First Amendment of the U.S. Constitution.

The result of this decision was a deluge of monetary contributions flooding the American political system. It led to the creation of what is now known as the super PAC, which refers to a group of like-minded citizens who come together to support or oppose a candidate or cause, raise money, and promote their interests through advertising or other means.

Super PACs are not bound by contribution limits and are able to accept donations from corporations and unions. They have this freedom because they operate independently of candidates and parties, and are not allowed to coordinate their spending with these entities. Nevertheless, it is not hard to see how super PACs could abuse the system and get around these restrictions. Dark money contributions, for example, where the donor is unknown, have increased dramatically in the post-*Citizens United* era. Such donors can now spend large sums to influence American elections. Experts estimate that in the presidential election year of 2020 well over a billion dollars in dark money flooded the American political system.

As with any controversial issue, debate around the *Citizens United* decision has continued to rage since the Supreme Court verdict. Seeking a way around the Supreme Court decision, some groups have called for a constitutional amendment to ban dark money and close campaign finance loopholes. A group called American Promise has proposed a 28th Amendment (there are currently 27) to do just this. Regarding their proposal, American Promise offers this statement:

> 86% of Americans think the influence of money in politics is the major threat to democracy, and solving this issue has supermajority support from all Americans across the political spectrum. It is one of the top 4 issues Americans want Congress to address right now.
>
> American Promise was founded to solve this problem once and for all by passing the For Our Freedom constitutional amendment—so we can set reasonable limits on campaign spending and restore the voice of the American People.[1]

Despite its noble intentions, it is unlikely that American Promise—or any other group—can help tighten up finance laws. The hurdles for creating a new amendment are so high that passage of such a law in a highly divided political landscape would be a monumental task. Moreover, for every group trying to rein in current campaign finance laws, there are opposing groups who are just as dogged in their determination to maintain—or even expand—corporate donations and dark money contributions to political candidates.

Notes

1. " The Tipping Point for Change," https://americanpromise.net/.

Viewpoint 1

> *"After a decade of data, research shows that the candidate who has more money, wins more often."*

The *Citizens United* Decision Changed Political Spending

Nick Bentley

In this viewpoint, Nick Bentley provides an overview of Citizens United, *the nickname given to the court case that overhauled the U.S. system of political donations. The Supreme Court's decision in favor of loosening laws regarding how organizations can finance political campaigns has had a dramatic effect on political spending. Bentley's organization, Reclaim Democracy, opposes the court decision, arguing that injecting so much money into campaigns threatens our political system, making dollars more important than ideas. For Bentley,* Citizens United *isn't an isolated problem, but a symptom of a bigger threat: corporations are gaining more power over government at the expense of individual citizens. Nick Bentley is an organizer at Reclaim Democracy, an organization that works toward a more democratic republic, where citizens play an active role in shaping their communities, states, and nation.*

As you read, consider the following questions:

1. What reasons did the Supreme Court's majority give for siding with Citizens United?

"What Is Citizens United? An Introduction," by Nick Bentley, Reclaim Democracy. Reprinted by permission.

2. What dissenting opinions did the court's minority voter offer?
3. What reasons does Bentley give for Reclaim Democracy's opposition to the *Citizens United* decision?

What is Citizens United? The short answer is it's two different but related things: a Political Action Committee (PAC) in Washington, D.C., and a Supreme Court case about election spending in which the aforementioned PAC was the plaintiff. Both lie at the center of a debate over the role corporations play in society. Read on for the long answer.

It's a Political Action Committee

Citizens United, the PAC, was founded in 1988 by Floyd Brown, a longtime Washington political consultant, with major funding from the Koch brothers (industrialists who own "the second largest privately owned company in the United States"). The group promotes corporate interests, socially conservative causes and candidates who advance their goals, which it says are "...limited government, freedom of enterprise, strong families, and national sovereignty and security." It gained fame in 2009 for suing the Federal Election Commission, leading to a controversial Supreme Court case (now also commonly known as *Citizens United)* eliminating some restrictions on how corporations can spend money in elections.

It's a Supreme Court Case

In the 2008 election season, Citizens United the PAC sought to broadcast TV ads for a video-on-demand film criticizing presidential candidate Hillary Rodham Clinton, but doing so would violate the 2002 Bipartisan Campaign Reform Act (known also as the McCain–Feingold Act), which barred corporations and unions from paying for media that mentioned any candidate in periods immediately preceding elections.

Citizens United challenged the law, suing the Federal Election Commission (which sets campaign finance laws and election rules), and the case made its way through lower courts until an appeal was granted by the U.S. Supreme Court.

In a 5-4 ruling, the justices declared unconstitutional the government restriction on "independent" political spending by corporations and unions, and determined the anti-Clinton broadcast should have been allowed. The decision overturned century-old precedent allowing the government to regulate such spending. As a result, *Citizens United* has greatly affected the way corporations and unions can spend on elections (more on that below).

The Court majority (Justices Kennedy, Roberts, Alito, Scalia, and Thomas) argued:

1. barring independent political spending amounts to squelching free speech protected by the First Amendment.
2. the First Amendment protects not just a person's right to speak, but the act of speech itself, regardless of the speaker. Therefore the First Amendment protects the speech of corporations and unions, whether we consider them people or not.
3. although government has the authority to prevent corruption or "the appearance of corruption," it has no place in determining whether large political expenditures are either of those things, so it may not impose spending limits on that basis.
4. the public has the right to hear all available information, and spending limits prevent information from reaching the public.

The Court minority (Justices Stevens, Ginsburg, Breyer, and Sotomayor) argued:

1. the First Amendment protects only individual speech.
2. government may prevent corruption, and campaign spending can be corrupt when it buys influence over

legislators. Therefore government may impose spending limits on corporations and unions.

3. government may prevent the appearance of corruption, which undermines public confidence in democracy. Limits

How *Citizens United* Changed Politics

Since the U.S. Supreme Court ruled, in 2010, that corporations and labor unions can spend freely on political advertisements, unprecedented amounts of money have poured into American elections.

Who has benefited from the influx of cash? Overwhelmingly, the Republican Party, according to new research by Columbia political scientist Carlo Prato. He and Nour Abdul-Razzak, of the University of Chicago, and Stephane Wolton, of the London School of Economics and Political Science, recently conducted one of the first studies to quantify the effects of the *Citizens United* ruling on election outcomes. After comparing the results of state legislative elections held between 1990 and 2015, the researchers found that in the 23 states that formerly restricted corporate and union political spending, Republicans have won a three-to-four-point greater share of the vote since 2010 than would otherwise have been expected, given national voting trends. Not surprisingly, this appears to have won the GOP many tight races: the party's share of legislative seats in these states has jumped by an average of 5 percent.

In states with many powerful corporations and relatively low union membership, such as Texas, Mississippi, Idaho, and North and South Carolina, the *Citizens United* ruling appears to have increased Republican seat share by as much as 12 points. In states with high union membership, such as California, New York, Illinois, and Pennsylvania, the case has had no discernible effect on the partisan balance of legislatures.

"In many states, Democrats are getting crushed," Prato says. "In those with strong unions, they are merely holding their own."

"How 'Citizens United' Changed Our Politics," by David J. Craig, Columbia University, 2017.

on corporate and union political spending are an expression of that authority.

4. the public has the right to hear all available information, and when corporations spend money individuals can't match, messages from corporations drown out messages from others, and that information fails to reach the public.

Initial Public Response

The decision was controversial and set off a ferocious debate which continues to this day.

Effects of *Citizens United*

Spending was on the rise even before *Citizens United*, but the post-decision increase was dramatic. The 2012 presidential election was the first following *Citizens United*, with more than twice the political spending as any previous election. Independent political spending of the kind *Citizens United* allows accounted for all of that increase.

Is this new determining the winners of elections? Yes, after a decade of data, research shows that the candidate who has more money, wins more often.

What's Reclaim Democracy's Position?

We oppose the Court's *Citizens United* ruling, for the following reasons:

1. Given the strong restrictions our country's founders imposed on corporate activities, they clearly didn't intend for corporations to enjoy constitutional protections.
2. The government has the authority to prevent corruption or the appearance of it, but the *Citizens United* majority opinion says the government has no right to decide whether independent political spending drives those things. We argue government *can't* prevent corruption without the ability to identify the causes. This isn't just a theoretical

problem, because evidence suggests both government-corporate relations appear corrupt to the electorate, and those relations are *in fact* corrupt.

3. The majority's claim that spending limits prevent full information from reaching the public ignores reality. We're bombarded by information. We register only a fraction of it, and money (spent on advertising and promotions) strongly determines what ends up in that fraction. When wealthy groups can spend whatever they want, they can make sure their messaging drowns out other voices and limits the information reaching the public.
4. The Court had to overturn one of its own decisions to decide *Citizens United* as it did. The Court normally honors a custom called *Stare Decisis,* which means it tries not to overturn its own decisions if it can avoid doing so, by deciding a case on narrower grounds. In this case, the path was clear: the Court could have ruled the McCain-Feingold law doesn't apply to video-on-demand, a decision which would have aligned better with previous decisions. The Justices went far beyond what Citizens United's own lawyers asked for!

Beyond the legal objections, unlimited political spending by corporations and unions causes several problems:

1. It prevents a "meritocracy of ideas." Unlimited political spending allows ideas to dominate not by merit, but by their supporters' ability to broadcast them.
2. It has influence far beyond the ads it pays for. The more money a politician needs to compete for office, the more she must court the wealthy, leaving less time to govern and less contact with average citizens. Another consequence is that legislators' lives get tied up with wealthy supporters in ways that have led to widespread corruption in both parties.
3. The kind of unlimited political spending *Citizens United* allows (mostly on attack ads) creates a crude,

counterproductive form of political dialogue, which breeds unthinking partisanship and oversimplified discussion via sound bytes. We need to create a culture in which thoughtful political discussion can flourish, but the unregulated flood of money that *Citizens United* unleashed makes it harder to do so.

4. It gives large corporations anti-competitive advantages over small businesses.

We believe citizens and their elected representatives must have the right to limit the influence of money on candidates and elections in order to protect the integrity of elections and government. This includes the ability to implement public financing systems that match private spending.

The Big Picture

Citizens United isn't an isolated problem. It's a symptom of a bigger, longstanding threat: for decades the largest corporations have been building power over our political process—power that comes at the expense of citizens.

One of the main instruments of this influence is the legal concept of "corporate personhood," wherein corporations receive the same Constitutional protections as individuals. Corporations use these protections to claim the "right" to lie to the public, for example, or to influence elections in various ways. Corporations have lobbied for and received these protections for decades, despite our country's founders intending no such thing.

An important note: *Citizens United* isn't technically an extension of corporate personhood. The Court majority didn't say corporations have free speech rights because they're people, but instead stated non-persons have free speech rights. If your toaster could talk, it would have those rights too.

The case clarified, however, that a Constitutional Amendment is the only way to strip corporations of "constitutional rights." Moreover, many kinds of electoral reform, such as public campaign financing that truly levels the playing field, are legal impossibilities without first amending the Constitution (as a subsequent Supreme Court decision on campaign finance vividly demonstrates). For these reasons, there's now a rapidly growing grassroots movement afoot to do so.

At the head of this movement is Move to Amend, a broad national coalition with more than 150 chapters nationwide and nearly 250,000 endorsers (Reclaim Democracy is a co-founder). More than 600 cities and towns have passed resolutions or ordinances calling to end corporate personhood or have serious efforts underway.

Even more impressive, 10 states now have passed measures in opposition to *Citizens United.* Most recently, Colorado and Montana voters did so in early November 2012. Montana's measure opposed not just *Citizens United* but also the Supreme Court's creations of corporate personhood and "money=speech" (*Buckley v Valeo*) and passed by an overwhelming 75%-25% margin.

VIEWPOINT 2

> *"The political ads of outside entities are even more likely to be negative and dishonest than political ads sponsored by candidates and parties."*

The *Citizens United* Decision Has Negatively Affected American Politics

Taylor Lincoln

Taylor Lincoln writes that until the Citizens United *decision, a fairly basic set of rules governed political contributions and expenditures. There were always abuses, but the system generally worked. The passage of* Citizens United *ushered in an era of unregulated outside entities funding political candidates and parties. This has caused elected officials to become increasingly more responsive to the desires of special interests rather than to their constituents. Lincoln extensively quotes Justice Anthony Kennedy, who wrote the majority opinion in the case, to display how Kennedy's rationale for deciding the case has proven to be faulty. He cites Kennedy's later admission that the law he voted in favor of was "not working the way it should." Lincoln concludes by noting that some states are working to offset the impact of* Citizens United. *Taylor Lincoln is Director of Research at Public Citizen's Congress Watch division. He has authored or co-authored numerous reports on subjects concerning regulations, health care, worker safety and political spending, among other topics.*

"Ten Years After Citizens United Nine Ways the U.S. Supreme Court's Ruling Has Eroded Democracy, and Its One Positive Outcome," by Taylor Lincoln, PublicCitizen, January 15, 2020. Reprinted by permission.

As you read, consider the following questions:

1. According to the viewpoint, what were Justice Kennedy's assumptions about how *Citizens United* would work?
2. According to Lincoln, how was Kennedy proven incorrect in these assumptions?
3. According to the viewpoint, what negative effects has the *Citizens United* decision had on American politics?

Before Jan. 21, 2010, there were some fairly basic, generally noncontroversial, rules for making political contributions or other expenditures to influence U.S. elections. Chiefly, the donor needed to be a person, and that person needed to be a citizen or permanent resident of the United States. These rules were only slightly different than the rules on voting eligibility.

Contributions of more than $200 to federal political committees were disclosed, and corporations and unions were prohibited from spending money from their treasuries for overt activities to influence elections.

There were abuses of the system. For years, political parties and outside groups evaded the prohibition on corporate and union money by using money from these sources to pay for sham issue ads that were actually intended to influence elections. Meanwhile, funding of elections was never representative of the electorate, as a whole.[1]

But, despite these shortcomings, the vast majority of the money flowing into the system was given by individuals, was disclosed and was subject to contribution limits.

All of that changed when the U.S. Supreme Court handed down its decision in *Citizens United v. FEC* in early 2010.[2] The court ruled that it was unconstitutional to prohibit corporations and unions from engaging directly in elections. Based on that decision, a U.S. federal court and the Federal Election Commission soon issued rulings permitting outside groups to accept unlimited contributions to influence elections.[3] This gave rise to unrestricted independent expenditure-only committees, otherwise known as super PACs.

Justice Anthony Kennedy, the author of the majority opinion in the court's 5-4 decision in *Citizens United*, justified the decision on two primary rationales. First, he assumed that spending activities by outside groups are inherently independent of the candidates or parties whose prospects the spending seeks to affect. Independent spending, Kennedy assumed, does not pose a risk of corrupting candidates.

Second, Kennedy assumed that the sources of money behind the new spending would be disclosed. Therefore, Kennedy put forth, voters would be able to evaluate political messages by unregulated outside entities based on the credibility of those who funded them.

Both of Kennedy's foundational assumptions were almost immediately proven wrong. The *Citizens United* decision predictably caused an explosion of electioneering spending by outside entities. But the percentage of outside electioneering entities keeping their donors secret also soared.

Kennedy's assumption that the spending would be "independent" was destined to fall apart from the very moment that the court issued the decision. That is because the decision bestowed advantages on outside entities over regulated campaign and party committees. This provided an incentive for those operating within the conventional campaign finance system to conspire with unregulated outside entities.

The result has been that unregulated outside entities often do the bidding of candidates and parties at the behest of those same candidates and parties. Meanwhile, a handful of multimillionaires and billionaires underwrite much of that bidding. The political ads of outside entities are even more likely to be negative and dishonest than political ads sponsored by candidates and parties.

Elected officials have grown ever more responsive to the desires of special interests rather than to their constituents. The failure of the U.S. government to face the existential challenge of the climate crisis, redress wealth inequality that is more severe than any time in the last hundred years, restrain pharmaceutical prices that lead one in six Americans to ration their prescriptions, expand health care to cover everyone, impose meaningful penalties on corporate criminals, and hold Wall Street accountable for crashing our economy all trace directly to the undue political influence of the corporate class, which was superpowered by *Citizens United.*

What follows is a summary of the results *Citizens United* has wrought.

Citizens United Unleashed Torrents of Outside Spending by Unregulated Groups

In the first congressional elections after the decision was issued, spending by outside entities was more than four times greater than in the previous congressional cycle ($309.8 million versus $69.6 million). Outside spending in the first presidential election after *Citizens United* was more than three times greater than in the previous presidential cycle ($1,038 billion versus $338.4 million). It has risen steadily ever since.

Citizens United Led to a Massive Increase in Anonymous Political Spending

One of the chief rationales forwarded by Justice Anthony Kennedy in the *Citizens United* decision was that modern technology enabled the prompt disclosure of the funders of electioneering expenditures, thereby allowing members to the public to evaluate the credibility of the organizations seeking to influence their votes.

"With the advent of the Internet, prompt disclosure of expenditures can provide shareholders and citizens with the information needed to hold corporations and elected officials accountable for their positions and supporters," Kennedy wrote. "Shareholders can determine whether their corporation's political speech advances the corporation's interest in making profits, and citizens can see whether elected officials are 'in the pocket' of so-called moneyed interests."[4]

In reality, the law provided no assurance at the time Kennedy wrote those words that such disclosure would occur. In fact, the Kennedy had joined in a court decision about three years earlier that significantly reduced the likelihood of disclosure.

Congress had earlier in the decade passed a law that prohibited corporations or unions from funding advertisements depicting candidates in the run up to elections.[5] The law required organizations running advertisements to reveal the funders behind them. But in 2007, the Supreme Court issued a decision that gutted the prohibition on corporate and union-funded ads depicting candidates.[6] The court's decision prompted the Federal Election Commission to eliminate requirements that organizations disclose who funded their political messages.[7]

Disclosure plummeted after the 2007 Supreme Court decision and even more after it issued *Citizens United*. Public Citizen documented this trend in 2010. Whereas more than 95 percent of groups airing electioneering communications in the 2004 and 2006 election cycles disclosed their donors, disclosure fell to less than 50 percent in 2008 and to just above 30 percent in the 2010 election cycle. Electioneering communications are messages that mention candidates but do not explicitly urge voters to vote a certain way. Disclosure for independent expenditures, which do expressly advocate for candidates, was higher than for electioneering communications in 2010 but still significantly lower than in previous election cycles.

Subsequent election cycles have seen a proliferation in undisclosed spending, and in the methods by which groups avoid disclosing who is funding them.

In his *Citizens United* decision, Justice Kennedy assumed that shareholders would be able to assess the wisdom of their corporations' spending on elections. In fact, corporations are not obliged to share that information, and many resist calls to do so. Meanwhile, 501(c) nonprofit organizations that are active in elections and funded by contributions from corporations, such as the U.S. Chamber of Commerce, have strenuously fought proposals that they be required to disclose their donors' identities. The U.S. Chamber has spent about $30 million in each election cycle except one since 2010.[8]

Justice Kennedy acknowledged in an interview in 2016 that "disclosure is not working the way it should."[9]

Full disclosure, even if it were to exist, would be insufficient to enable voters to hold elected officials accountable for the distorting effects of large contributions by special interests. That said, if disclosure were to occur in the manner that Kennedy envisioned, government watchdogs could use the available data from this type of transparency to begin to hold bad actors accountable.

We do not know what is being kept from public scrutiny. Common sense suggests that the contributions kept in the shadows are the ones that would be most likely to arouse the public's suspicions about improper influences. Otherwise, why go so far to hide them?

Much of the New Spending that *Citizens United* Permitted Contradicted the Court's Assumption that Outside Spending Is Inherently "Independent" of Candidates and Parties

The primary basis on which the Supreme Court has traditionally upheld the constitutionality of limiting political contributions is the court's view that unrestricted contributions would pose an unacceptable risk of corrupting public officials and, relatedly, cause the public to lose faith in democratic institutions.

In *Citizens United*, the court opined that electioneering expenditures by outside entities do not pose enough risk of corrupting public officials to warrant restricting them.

In explaining his rationale, Justice Kennedy invoked language that the court had used in its landmark 1976 campaign finance opinion, *Buckley v. Valeo*. In that decision, the court wrote of independent expenditures that "the absence of prearrangement and coordination of an expenditure with the candidate or his agent not only undermines the value of the expenditure to the candidate, but also alleviates the danger that expenditures will be given as a quid pro quo for improper commitments from the candidate."[10]

This language assumed that expenditures legally categorized as "independent expenditures" truly are independent under the English definition of the word, thus lacking prearrangement and coordination with candidates.

Prior to the issuance of the *Citizens United* decision, outside entities likely did act in a largely independent fashion. That is because the rules governing the electioneering activities of outside entities were about the same as the rules governing candidate committees. But by lifting restrictions on outside entities, *Citizens United* created a strong incentive for restricted entities—like candidates and political parties—to collaborate with unregulated outside entities.

Candidates and parties quickly acted on those incentives. By the 2012 election cycle, outside entities that invested all their electioneering efforts to assist just a single candidate accounted for nearly 50 percent of all the unregulated outside entities seeking to influence elections, Public Citizen documented.[11]

While the phenomenon of an entity working on behalf of a single candidate does not, in itself, prove that it is not acting independently, it is highly suggestive of collaboration. Abundant anecdotal evidence has confirmed suspicions that many of these single-candidate groups are not truly independent. Instead, they tend to be operated by former staffers of the candidate.[12]

The 2012 election cycle also saw the advent of outside entities created by parties' congressional leadership teams to advance their parties' interests. These quasi-party-sponsored entities came in various forms, including super PACs that reveal most of their donors and 501(c) groups that reveal none.

While outside groups allied with a national party accounted for only 4 percent of outside spending entities in 2012, they accounted for 29 percent of spending by outside entities.

These trends have continued in the ensuing election cycles.

Thus, *Citizens United* created a contradictory legal landscape. The court in *Citizens United* left intact—and even affirmed—its support for campaign finance restrictions. "We must give weight to attempts by Congress to seek to dispel either the appearance or the reality" of improper influences, Justice Anthony Kennedy wrote in *Citizens United*.[13]

But by lifting restrictions on outside spending, the court created a situation in which Congress may limit contributions to candidates but may not act to stop a super PAC established by the candidate's best friend from accepting a contribution of unlimited size.

U.S. Court of Appeals Judge Richard Posner, widely regarded as a conservative jurist, expressed the view that the current landscape is contradictory. It "is difficult to see what practical difference there is between super PAC donations and direct campaign donations, from a corruption standpoint," Posner wrote in April 2012. "A super PAC is a valuable weapon for a campaign… ; the donors to it are known; and it is unclear why they should expect less quid pro quo from their favored candidate if he's successful than a direct donor to the candidate's campaign would be."[14]

Citizens United Empowered a Very Small Number of Super Rich Donors, and, More Generally, White Donors

A very small number of donors is responsible for a dominant share of the outside election spending unleashed by *Citizens United*. A new Public Citizen analysis finds that just 25 ultra-wealthy donors have made up nearly half (47 percent) of all individual contributions to super PACs since 2010, giving $1.4 billion of $2.96 billion in individual super PAC contributions. The top 100 donors are responsible for 60 percent of all super PAC contributions.

The top five donors, alone, account for more than a quarter of all super PAC contributions. They are: Republican casino billionaire Sheldon Adelson and his wife Miriam; hedge fund billionaire Tom Steyer and former New York Mayor Michael Bloomberg, Democratic presidential candidates; Richard and Elizabeth Uihlein, a Republican donor and president of a packaging company; and Fred Eychaner, a Democratic donor who owns a printing and media company.

Reflecting the enormous racial wealth gap in the United States, the vast majority of funding for super PACs comes from majority-white zip codes. Super PAC contributions from the top donating majority-white zip codes outpace those from the top donating majority-minority zip codes by more than 10-1.

Citizens United Facilitated More than Half a Billion Dollars in Corporate Contributions to Influence Elections

The bulk of money flowing into super PACs and outside spending entities post-*Citizens United* has come from the super wealthy—but corporations also have made enormous contributions, much of it obscured by their reliance on dark money conduits. A new Public Citizen analysis finds that, since the 2010 *Citizens United* decision, corporations at minimum have spent more than half a billion dollars to influence elections. More than 2,200 corporations reported $313 million on election-related spending, primarily contributions to super PACs. Additionally, 30 corporate trade groups, which do not disclose their donors, have spent $226 million for the purpose of influencing elections. That totals more $539 million in political spending—which is almost surely an undercount because it does not count corporate contributions to dark money 501(c)(4) social welfare organizations.

As with contributions from individuals, a small number of corporate contributors are responsible for a disproportionate amount of total spending. The top 20 corporate donors account for $118 million—more than a third—of corporate donations reported to the Federal Election Commission. These entities donated exclusively to super PACs that back Republicans. Only four of these top corporate donors are publicly traded. Three are energy corporations—Chevron, NextEra Energy and Pinnacle West Capital—and the fourth is a subsidiary of British American

Tobacco. Twenty of the top corporate donors have executives, chairpersons or other top figures who have who also have donated generously to political campaigns.

The U.S. Chamber of Commerce is, by far, the most consequential of the nondisclosing corporate trade groups. It has spent $143 million—nearly two-thirds of the total election-related spending by corporate trade associations.

Citizens United Provided a Pathway for Foreign Entities to Influence U.S. Elections

One of the concerns that Justice John Paul Stevens raised in his dissent to the majority opinion in *Citizens United* was that the new regime would permit people and corporations from foreign countries to make expenditures to influence elections. Such activities are banned by federal law. But "unlike voters in U.S. elections, corporations may be foreign controlled," Stevens wrote.

Direct spending by foreign corporations is not the only way that foreign interests might influence elections under the post-*Citizens United* landscape. Foreign interests, including individuals, also may contribute to super PACs in the name of front companies.

The Intercept in 2017 reported on four cases in which foreign nationals and foreign-controlled corporations contributed seven figure sums to super PACs.[15]One of those instances involved a company controlled by a Chinese couple making a $1.3 million contribution to a super PAC supporting Jeb Bush.

The contribution was discussed ahead of time between one of the Chinese donors and Jeb Bush's brother, Neil, who was on the board of the company controlled by the Chinese nationals. Neil Bush had indicated in an e-mail to the executive director of the Chinese-held company that its owners had "expressed interest in donating legally through APIC to my brother Jeb's political action committee."[16] This anecdote is notable not only because it reflected Neil Bush's awareness of the potential legal issues, but because Bush refers to the committee in question as being connected to his brother. As a matter of law, and as envisioned in *Citizens United*, Jeb Bush was prohibited from having anything to do with the super PAC.

After *The Intercept* revealed details about case, the Federal Election Commission investigated and, four years later, fined the super PAC and the donors nearly $1 million.[17]

But resolutions like that rely on incriminating details emerging. In 2016, *The Washington Post* documented the phenomenon of ghost corporations, often limited liability corporations, contributing to super PACs. There is often no meaningful information about the people behind these LLCs, let alone the funders of them. These leaves little ability for investigators to detect if their donors include foreign contributors.

The current system leaves plenty of opportunities for outside entities to keep those details hidden, and thus, we do not know the extent of foreign contributions flowing into outside electioneering groups.

Citizens United Encouraged More and More Negative Advertising

Americans have long lamented the negative ads, or attack ads, that dominate the airwaves in the run up to closely contested elections. These ads often demonize candidates in ways that bear little resemblance to reality.

Candidates face a potential backlash for airing these ads because voters might penalize them for polluting the airwaves. But outside entities, especially ones that voters know little or nothing about, do not face these sort of risks. Studies have confirmed that voters are less likely to penalize candidates for attack ads issued by unknown groups.[18]

In the 2012 elections, advertisements aired by outside groups backing the major party candidates were significantly more likely to be negative than those aired by the candidates themselves, Public Citizen's analysis of data provided by the Wesleyan Media Project showed. For instance, the share of ads by outside groups backing Republican nominee Mitt Romney that were negative was

89 percent, compared to 49 percent for those put out by Romney's campaign.[19]

In 2018, a fact checker for the *Washington Post* assessed six randomly selected advertisements sponsored by the Congressional Leadership Fund, a super PAC that is allied with the Republican House leadership. "For all six ads, we found that the Congressional Leadership Fund took a sliver of accurate information and spun it in a misleading way," the *Post* reporter wrote. "Even by modern mudslinging standards, these ads by the Congressional Leadership Fund stand out for their dark tone and their strained relationship with the facts."[20]

Citizens United Left Local Entities, Even Those as Small as School Systems, Powerless Against an Avalanche of Outside Money

The rules left behind by *Citizens United* do not only affect federal elections. They prohibit state and local officials from placing limitations on spending to influence elections, as well. This dynamic is potentially even more destabilizing than for federal elections because the amounts that are ordinarily spent in local elections are much smaller.

Public Citizen in 2014 documented instances in which Americans for Prosperity, the advocacy group controlled by billionaire Charles Koch, sought to influence elections in small towns. In Iron County, Wis., for instance, Americans for Prosperity campaigned against candidates who opposed a proposed open pit iron mine. [21]

Candidates for the county's Board of Supervisors had traditionally run unopposed. For the 2014 election in which Americans for Prosperity became involved, however, 10 of the 15 contests were contested. Americans for Prosperity sent out mailers to 1,000 homes denouncing candidates opposing the mine as "anti-mining radicals."[22]

Big cities' campaign finance systems can be turned upside down by *Citizens United*, as well. For instance, in 2014, a high-ranking official in the Chicago school system left her post to assume the reins of a super PAC that would support Chicago Mayor Rahm Emanuel and other candidates allied with Emanuel.

The former Chicago schools official said of super PAC, "they're the shiny new object in campaigns today, and they provide new flexibility—especially in municipalities and states where there's far more stringent control."[23] She later touted on her LinkedIn page that the Chicago super PAC "raised $5 million to fund the development and implementation of paid media campaigns in support of Mayor Rahm Emanuel's reelection and 35 aldermanic elections. More than 70% of its supported candidates won election or reelection to the Chicago City Council."[24]

Citizens United Led to Further Erosions of Campaign Finance Laws

Significant, additional erosions to campaign finance laws followed the *Citizens United* decision.

Shortly after the *Citizens United* decision, a U.S. circuit court and the Federal Election Commission issued rulings permitting outside groups to accept unlimited contributions to influence elections.[25]

These rulings significantly broadened the impact of *Citizens United*. Whereas, Justice Kennedy envisioned the *Citizens United* decision permitting existing, known corporations to spend to influence elections, the follow up rulings enabled entities to be created overnight with little more paper trail than a Post Office box to accept unlimited—sometimes undisclosed—contributions to influence elections.

In 2013, the U.S. Supreme Court in *McCutcheon v. FEC* struck down limits on the aggregate amount of money that individuals could contribute to federal candidates and political parties.[26] At the time of the decision, individuals were limited to contributing no more than $123,000 per two-year cycle to all federal candidates and committees.[27]

The court's rationale was that campaign contribution limits are intended to prevent a donor from obtaining improper favor from a given candidate. The court's 5-4 majority based its decision on a belief that a person giving contributions to an unlimited number of candidates was not more potentially corrupting provided that no single candidate received more than the maximum amount.

Of course, if a person were to give to the entirety of a party's congressional caucus and to all of its party committees, that person would likely be received more favorably by elected officials than an ordinary citizen. Many people might conclude that such an outcome would constitute corruption, but Chief Justice John Roberts, writing for the majority, did not. He reached that conclusion by adopting a particularly narrow definition of "corruption."

"Ingratiation and access ... are not corruption," John Roberts wrote in *McCutcheon*, citing *Citizens United*. "[W]hile preventing corruption or its appearance is a legitimate objective, Congress may target only a specific type of corruption—'quid pro quo' corruption."[28]

Roberts' defined "quid quo pro" as a "direct exchange of an official act for money."

In dissent, Justice Stephen Breyer disputed Roberts' characterization that the court, before *Citizens United*, had deemed only direct "quid pro quo" exchanges as constituting corruption. Breyer also disputed Roberts' view it was proper to draw the line at "quid pro quo" exchanges. Breyer wrote that the court had in the past "used the phrase 'subversion of the political process' to describe circumstances in which '[e]lected officials are influenced to act contrary to their obligations of office by the prospect of financial gain to themselves or infusions of money into their campaigns.' "[29]

About eight months after the *McCutcheon* decision was issued, Congress without debate in 2014 inserted a provision in a budget deal that dramatically expanded the amounts of money that individuals could give to party committees, by some estimates, from about $97,000 a year to about $777,000 year.[30]Although the increase was not officially made in response to *Citizens United*, the congressional leaders who negotiated it likely justified it on the basis that *Citizens United* had given an advantage to outside groups over political parties.

Citizens United Gave Rise to a Growing Pro-Democracy Movement

The American public strongly disapproves of *Citizens United.* Polling has consistently showed overwhelming opposition to the decision among those who identify as Republican, Democrat or Independent/Other. Polling consistently shows 9 in 10 Americans expressing disgust with Big Money influence in politics and three quarters or more of Americans supporting a constitutional amendment to overturn *Citizens United.*[31] Reviewing poll results, a *Bloomberg* writer in 2015 noted, "Americans may be sharply divided on other issues, but they are united in their view of the 2010 Supreme Court ruling that unleashed a torrent of political spending: They hate it."[32] Americans across the political spectrum want far-reaching solutions to the *Citizens United*-enabled flood of Big Money in politics. "With near unanimity," reported *The New York Times*, "the public thinks the country's campaign finance system needs significant changes." Americans are roughly split between whether the system needs "fundamental change" (39 percent) or should be "completely rebuil[t]" (46 percent); effectively no one believes no changes are needed.[33]

That profound disgust with *Citizens United* has fueled an ever-growing democracy movement. Thanks to that movement, 20 states and more than 800 localities have passed resolutions calling for a constitutional amendment to overturn the decision. Millions have signed petitions calling for an amendment. In 2014, the U.S. Senate voted 54-45 in favor a constitutional amendment. More than 200 Members of the House of Representatives have co-sponsored a constitutional amendment in the current Congress.

Citizens have focused as well on confronting dark money and forcing disclosure of secret campaign spending. More than

1 million people have submitted comments to the Securities and Exchange Commission in support of a petition calling for a rule requiring publicly traded companies to disclose their political spending.[34]

The movement has also scored some legislative successes. In March 2019, the U.S. House of Representatives passed H.R. 1, the For the People Act, the most sweeping pro-democracy legislation in the past 50 years. Among other measures, in the campaign finance space, it would provide for small donor and public financing of elections, tighten rules on super PACs, end dark money, and much more. H.R. 1 also includes other pro-democracy measures, including automatic voter registration, restoration of voting rights for people convicted of felonies who have served their time, addressing gerrymandering and more.[35] A huge coalition of organizations, known as the Declaration for American Democracy, backs H.R. 1.[36]

Meanwhile, thanks to prodding from the growing democracy movement, cities and states have pursued aggressive measures to offset the impact of *Citizens United*, with Washington, D.C.; Seattle; Montgomery County, Maryland; New York State; among others, adopting public financing systems in recent years. Countless other states and localities have adopted disclosure rules, contribution limits and other reforms.[37]

Footnotes

[1] See, for example, *The Color of Money*, Public Campaign (2001), http://bit.ly/2uGAnNF.

[2] *Citizens United v. Federal Election Commission*, 130 S.Ct. 876 (2010), http://bit.ly/30ramxJ.

[3] See, *SpeechNow.org v. Federal Election Commission*, 599 F.3d 686 (D.C. Cir. 2010), http://bit.ly/3abXdgo and Federal Election Commission, Advisory Opinion 2010-11 (July 22, 2010), http://bit.ly/lK6LUX.

[4] *Citizens United v. Federal Election Commission*, 130 S.Ct. 876 (2010), http://bit.ly/30ramxJ.

[5] Bipartisan Campaign Reform Act of 2002, http://bit.ly/2ReqjTT.

[6] *Federal Election Commission v. Wisconsin Right to Life*, 551 U.S. 449 (2007), http://bit.ly/30in8i6

[7] 11 CFR 104.20(c)(9), http://bit.ly/2ReqjTT.

[8] See spending by outside groups documented by the Center for Responsive Politics, 2010 forward, starting here, http://bit.ly/2Rlc1Re.

[9] Eliza Newlin Carney, *Citizens United Fuels Movement for Overhaul*, American Prospect (Jan. 21, 2016), http://bit.ly/2tVhMNJ.
[10] *Buckley v. Valeo*, 424 U.S. 1 (1976), http://bit.ly/2t8VpV3.
[11] Taylor Lincoln, *Super Connected*, Public Citizen (March 2013), http://bit.ly/3aa2Ziy.
[12] *Id.*
[13] *Citizens United v. Federal Election Commission*, 130 S.Ct. 876 (2010), http://bit.ly/30ramxJ.
[14] Richard Posner, *Unlimited Campaign Spending—A Good Thing?* The Becker-Posner Blog (April 8, 2012), http://bit.ly/S1c8xU.
[15] Jon Schwarz, *John Paul Stevens Was Right: Citizens United Opened The Door To Foreign Money In U.S. Elections*, The Intercept (July 19, 2019), http://bit.ly/36UCeNe.
[16] Nihal Krishan, *Election Watchdog Hits Jeb Bush's Super-PAC With Massive Fine for Taking Money From Foreign Nationals*, Mother Jones (March 11, 2019), http://bit.ly/36Vz4st.
[17] Michelle Ye Hee Lee, *Pro-Jeb Bush super PAC improperly accepted $1.3 million from Chinese-owned company, FEC says*, The Washington Post, (March 11, 2019), https://wapo.st/2Ru7zzZ .
[18] Deborah Jordan Brooks and Michael Murov, *Assessing Accountability in a Post-Citizens United Era: The Effects of Attack Ad Sponsorship by Unknown Independent Groups*, American Politics Research (April 23, 2012), http://bit.ly/2thCAij and Conor M. Dowling and Amber Wichowsky, *Attacks without Consequence? Candidates, Parties, Groups, and the Changing Face of Negative Advertising*, American Journal of Political Science (March 21, 2014), http://bit.ly/3abSRG4.
[19] Adam Crowther, *Citizens United Fuels Negative Spending*, Public Citizen (Nov. 2, 2012), http://bit.ly/385ciOZ .
[20] Salvador Rizzo, *Fact-checking Republican attack ads in tight House races*, Washington Post (Aug. 31, 2018),
https://wapo.st/383Y8xE.
[21] Adam Crowther, *Outside Spenders, Local Elections*, Public Citizen (July 19, 2014), http://bit.ly/2Nu5VNw.
[22] *Id.*
[23] Theodore Schleifer, *Super PACs coming to a city near you*, CNN Politics (May 19, 2015), http://cnn.it/2fIdDUF.
[24] Michael Tanglis, *The Foundation of Citizens United Is in Ruins*, Public Citizen (March 17, 2017), http://bit.ly/2uQwcPB.
[25] *See*, See, *SpeechNow.org v. Federal Election Commission*, 599 F.3d 686 (D.C. Cir. 2010), http://bit.ly/3abXdgo and Federal Election Commission, Advisory Opinion 2010-11 (July 22, 2010), http://bit.ly/lK6LUX.
[26] *McCutcheon Et al. v. Federal Election Commission*, 572 US 185 (2014), http://bit.ly/2QT1spB.
[27] Contribution limits for 2013-2014, Federal Election Commission, http://bit.ly/2TuPxjH.
[28] *McCutcheon Et al. v. Federal Election Commission*, 572 US 185 (2014), http://bit.ly/2QT1spB.
[29] *Id.*
[30] Kenneth P. Vogel, *The man behind the political cash grab: A powerful Democratic lawyer crafted the campaign finance deal*, Politico (Dec. 12, 2014), https://politi.co/3a37Lym .

[31] *A Survey of Voters Nationwide*, Voice of the People (May 2018), http://bit.ly/3acPIpo. See additional polling here: https://democracyisforpeople.org/page.cfm?id=7.

[32] Greg Stohr, *Bloomberg Poll: Americans Want Supreme Court to Turn Off Political Spending Spigot*

Americans are divided on the justices' decisions on gay marriage, health care, and abortion. But not on campaign finance, Bloomberg (Sept. 28, 2015), https://bloom.bg/3aaLkYc.

[33] *The New York Times-CBS News Poll: 'Americans' Views on Money in Politics,'* The New York Times (June 2, 2015), https://nyti.ms/3abpUu7.

[34] Comments on Rulemaking Petition: Petition to require public companies to disclose to shareholders the use of corporate resources for political activities [File No. 4-637], Securities and Exchange Commission, http://bit.ly/2TpwJlC.

[35] *See,* The For the People Act, http://bit.ly/2RkL68p.

[36] *See,* Declaration for American Democracy, https://declarationforamericandemocracy.org/.

[37] Campaign Finance Legislation, 2015 Onward, National Conference of State Legislatures, http://bit.ly/2TpJDjQ.

Viewpoint 3

> *"This freewheeling political dialogue may be messy, imperfect, and prone to abuses, but the First Amendment makes it constitutionally preferable to censorship targeted at disfavored groups."*

Defending *Citizens United*

Anthony Dick

In this viewpoint, Anthony Dick considers the most common arguments against the Citizens United *decision and offers a refutation in each case. Dick's argument largely rests on the First Amendment, which guarantees freedom of speech to individuals. Since it takes money to broadcast one's speech to large groups, Dick defends this practice as well. Of course, he admits, "this freewheeling political dialogue may be messy, imperfect, and prone to abuses," but Dick's stance is that even these abuses are preferable to imposing censorship on groups that wish to spread their political opinions. Anthony Dick is an attorney and an associate editor at* National Review. *He served as a law clerk for Supreme Court Justice Samuel Alito.*

"Defending Citizens United," by Anthony Dick, National Review, January 25, 2010. Reprinted by permission.

As you read, consider the following questions:

1. How does Dick argue against the notion that *Citizens United* will radically increase powerful corporate influence in politics?
2. According to the viewpoint, why is the idea that corporate political expenditures violate shareholders' rights invalid?
3. How does Dick refute the idea that Republicans will be harmed by the *Citizens United* decision?

Bad arguments have been proliferating in the wake of this week's *Citizens United* case, which struck down restrictions on political expenditures by corporations and unions. The opinion leaves in place limits on campaign donations, but frees up corporations and unions to spend as much as they like to disseminate political messages. Here is a rogue's gallery of the most common arguments I've heard against the holding, followed by brief explanations of their profound misguidedness.

This 5–4 Decision Is a Blatant Example of Judicial Activism and Conservatives Are Hypocritical for Supporting It

Judicial activism occurs when judges abandon constitutional or statutory meaning and impose their policy preferences instead. A decision that faithfully applies the First Amendment is not activism but rather a proper exercise of the judicial responsibility to keep Congress within its constitutional bounds. The government argued in *Citizens United* that it had the power to outlaw books and movies produced by unions and corporations, both non-profit and for-profit, if they included even a single line addressing an election or a political issue. Such blatant censorship of core political speech falls well within the text and original meaning of the First Amendment, which supported an open marketplace of ideas by declaring in broad terms that "Congress shall make no law . . . abridging the freedom of speech." Contrast this with the paradigmatic examples of left-wing judicial activism, which have manufactured a host of "fundamental" rights without anything resembling such a clear textual basis.

Political Expenditures Are Not "Speech" and Should Not Be Protected Under the First Amendment

The force of this seductive argument evaporates upon the realization that spending money is an indispensable component of effective political speech, especially when it involves any audience above a trivial size. If the government could ban expenditures related to speech, it could easily circumvent the First Amendment simply by targeting the necessary funding underlying any communication. Imagine the *New York Times* being prohibited from paying for its writers, production, advertising, and distribution. Wonderful as this might sound in some of its particulars, you can see how the paper's right to free expression might be crimped. And so it goes for any person or group wishing to disseminate a political message through print or broadcast media, which is why the Court has properly subsumed the right to political expenditures within the right to free speech.

The Protections of the Free Speech Clause Properly Apply Only to Individuals, Not Corporations

Justice Scalia dispatched with this argument nicely in his concurring opinion by pointing out that the First Amendment has long been extended beyond isolated individuals to groups and associations whose members gather for a wide variety of purposes ranging from political to commercial. The Democratic party, the Sierra Club, and the *New York Times* aren't individuals, but their speech nonetheless falls under the umbrella of First Amendment protection. But the formalistic obsession with whether a corporation should have the legal status of a "person" with a "right" to free speech quite misses the substantive issues at stake, which concern how the principle of free expression should be applied to the political speech of certain types of social groups. In particular, is there something uniquely harmful and/or unworthy of protection about political messages that come from corporations and unions, as opposed to, say, rich individuals, persuasive writers, or charismatic demagogues? Which brings us to our next point:

A Deluge of Corporate and Union Speech Will Corrupt the Democratic Process

The very idea that political speech in an open democracy can be "corrupting" rests on fundamentally illiberal assumptions about individuals' capacity for reasoned deliberation and self-government. The First Amendment was designed to allow all speakers to put their messages out into the public debate, be they rich or poor, vicious or virtuous. The underlying principle is that over the long run, a society of free individuals is best equipped to evaluate the merits of political arguments for themselves, and that a distrustful government cannot ban speech out of the worry that its citizens will be unduly swayed by it. Rich individuals and talented polemicists have always been permitted to put out quantities and qualities of speech that may exert a disproportionate influence on society, but political opponents and voters have always been trusted to evaluate these speakers' arguments for themselves, respond with counter-arguments, and ultimately make up their own minds about the truth of any matter of controversy. Especially with the explosion of diverse viewpoints and avenues of expression that have come from the Internet media revolution, it simply defies common sense to think that any corporation or union could ever hope to so overwhelm the political debate as to prevent dissenting voices from being heard and reasonably contemplated by the electorate. Of course, this freewheeling political dialogue may be messy, imperfect, and prone to abuses, but the First Amendment makes it constitutionally preferable to censorship targeted at disfavored groups.

This Decision Will Radically Increase Powerful Corporate Influence in Politics, Compared to the Status Quo

History and economics together suggest that powerful corporate interests operating under an extensive regulatory state will always find a way exert a strong influence in politics. Up until now, campaign-finance regulations have had two ugly impacts: First, they have imposed huge legal costs on those wishing to participate in the political process, effectively shutting out smaller voices who cannot afford to pay campaign lawyers and risk legal trouble in getting their messages across. Loosening legal restrictions on smaller businesses will now allow them to enter the marketplace of political ideas on a more equal footing with their larger competitors. Second, campaign-expenditure limits have driven corporate money away from public dialogue and into channels that have been more corrosive and less transparent (think lobbyists, lawsuits, and regulatory capture). While these more pernicious forms of corporate influence are not likely to disappear any time soon, they may be mitigated to the extent that corporations can now pursue their policy objectives through a more open, deliberative process.

Corporate Political Expenditures Violate Shareholders' Rights to Withhold Funds from Messages They Disagree With

Two problems here. First, like members of any free association, shareholders have an absolute and easy-to-exercise right to exit from any corporation—in this instance, by simply selling their shares and relocating their investments. It is true that mutual funds and retirement accounts can complicate things, but shareholders maintain the ultimate legal right of control over their assets, including initial investment decisions. In any event, the level of "message subsidy" involved in most of these cases will be so diffuse as to be negligible, especially when compared to government policies and messages that taxpayers must fund despite strong disagreement. Second, corporations commonly disseminate non-political messages and make corporate decisions, including charitable donations, that might strongly offend shareholders. This is tolerated as part of the trade-off inherent in the structure of corporate governance, wherein shareholders voluntarily surrender control of their companies' day-to-day operations in exchange for the efficiencies of corporate decision-making.

This Decision Will Harm Republicans by Rallying Public Opinion in Favor of Populist-Progressive Reform and Against the "Conservative" Supreme Court Majority that Decided the Case

While four members of the *Citizens United* majority might fairly be called conservatives, the actual author of the opinion was Justice Kennedy, who defies easy political categorization. In the past few years, he has been repeatedly toasted in liberal circles for penning such sweeping decisions as *Lawrence* v. *Texas* and *Kennedy v. Louisiana*, declaring a constitutional right to sodomy and forbidding the death penalty for non-homicidal child rape, respectively. At the very least, those opinions give him some credibility as an independent voice. But perhaps more importantly, a recent Gallup poll shows that a majority of the public actually agrees with the Court that corporations and unions should be treated just like individuals in terms of their political-expenditure rights, and that the government should not attempt to protect its citizens from hearing seductive messages put out by sinister, powerful interests.

Viewpoint 4

> *"We are left with a campaign finance system where wealthy special interests can use unlimited secret spending to drown out the voices of everyday Americans."*

The *Citizens United* Decision Has Made Campaign Finance Abuse Rampant

Georgia Lyon

Georgia Lyon writes about the ramifications of the Citizens United *decision in this viewpoint. She points out how the law is still affecting political campaigns and how, on a practical level, it has paved the way for independent groups to abuse the campaign finance system. The judges who ruled on* Citizens United *did not account for the outsized influence that independent groups would have on campaigns. Record amounts of money are now being spent on promoting candidates, and the individual citizen's voice is being drowned out. Georgia Lyon is a communications assistant at Campaign Legal Center. Campaign Legal Center advances democracy through law, fighting for every American's right to participate in and affect the democratic process.*

As you read, consider the following questions:

1. According to the viewpoint, why have campaign finance disclosure laws been abused with impunity?

"How Does the *Citizens United* Decision Still Affect Us in 2022?," by Georgia Lyon, Campaign Legal Center, January 21, 2022. Reprinted by permission.

2. How has campaign spending changed since 2008?
3. How did a group supporting Republican presidential candidate Carly Fiorina circumvent campaign finance laws?

Voters have a right to know which wealthy special interests are spending big money to influence our vote and our government to rig the political system in their favor, but as the 2022 midterm elections approach, a case decided by the U.S. Supreme Court 12 years ago continues to threaten that fundamental right.

On Jan. 21, 2010, in the case *Citizens United v. Federal Election Commission (FEC),* the Court ruled to strike down a prohibition on corporate independent expenditures, which has since enabled corporations and other outside groups to engage in unlimited amounts of campaign spending.

In *Citizens United,* the Court upheld certain disclosure provisions from the Bipartisan Campaign Reform Act (BCRA), reasoning that prompt disclosure would be enough to prevent wealthy special interests from dominating the political process because voters could see who was paying for the ads and "give proper weight to different speakers and messages."

The Court assumed that unlimited corporate campaign spending would pose no threat of corruption or the appearance of corruption because it would be "independent."

However, it has become clear in the years since that voters are not getting enough information about the true sources of campaign spending and this supposedly independent spending in support of candidates or their campaigns is often intentionally coordinated.

Thus, we are left with a campaign finance system where wealthy special interests can use unlimited secret spending to drown out the voices of everyday Americans.

One way this has occurred is through creation of super PACs, which can accept unlimited contributions from nearly any non-foreign source and spend unlimited amounts to influence the outcome of federal elections.

Super PACs are theoretically required to be transparent about where their money comes from by reporting their fundraising and spending to the FEC. But that transparency is undermined when super PACs report contributions from secretly funded "dark money" groups, which themselves keep their donors hidden from the public.

Simply knowing that a super PAC is mostly or entirely funded by a vaguely named group that doesn't disclose its funding denies voters crucial information.

This is a bipartisan problem. Major super PACs aligned with the leadership of both parties have received tens of millions of dollars, and in some cases most or all of their funding, from groups that keep their donors hidden from the public.

It has also become a growing problem as each respective election cycle has seen record-breaking amounts of spending. Campaign spending by corporations and other outside groups increased by nearly 900% between 2008 and 2016. In 2020, total election spending was $14.4 billion, up from $5.7 billion in 2018, and more than $1 billion in dark money was spent.

Additionally, even though it's illegal for outside groups to coordinate election spending with candidates or political parties, many do because by and large, the FEC has failed to crack down on candidates and super PACs that work hand-in-glove.

The prevalence of this practice shows how the Court's assumption in *Citizens United* that unlimited campaign spending would be conducted independently was erroneous.

For instance, supporters of Carly Fiorina established the super PAC "Carly for America" in the run-up to the 2016 presidential primary. "Carly for America" had almost the same name as her official campaign committee "Carly For President."

By signing up attendees of events for the super PAC's email list, handing out campaign stickers and helping with the setup prior to events, "Carly for America" maintained an active presence at most of Fiorina's campaign events and served functions traditionally filled by campaign staff.

While this instance was brazen, "Carly for America" is far from alone. Super PACs are routinely established by close former aides of candidates, often contracting with the same consultants as the campaigns they support and candidates regularly appear at fundraising events for their supportive super PACs.

Campaign Legal Center (CLC) has filed complaints against several Democratic and Republican-affiliated candidates and groups for violating illegal coordination laws in the years following the *Citizens United* ruling.

As the 2022 midterms approach, the *Citizens United* decision will likely once again enable record-breaking amounts of campaign spending, including large sums of dark money spending, which will be coordinated by candidates and their super PACs.

The main way we could mitigate the negative effects of this decision is by having Congress approve legislation to create stronger disclosure and trace-back requirements and address dysfunction at the FEC to make the agency more able to crack down on illegal coordination, protecting voters' right to know who is spending big money to influence their vote.

To allow voters to make their voices heard in our democracy, we need real transparency about who is spending big money on elections so that politicians can no longer receive unlimited secret money from wealthy special interests to support their campaigns.

Periodical and Internet Sources Bibliography

The following articles have been selected to supplement the diverse views presented in this chapter.

Ashley Balcerzak, "Study: Most Americans want to kill 'Citizens United' with constitutional amendment," the Center for Public Integrity, May 10, 2018. https://publicintegrity.org/politics/study-most-americans-want-to-kill-citizens-united-with-constitutional-amendment/.

Ryan Beck, "Why Citizens United Was a Reasonable Decision," July 3, 2020. https://www.ryanbeckauthor.com/2020/07/03/Why-Citizens-United-Was-a-Reasonable-Decision.html.

Sara Blackwell, "The Negative Impact of Citizens United And The Positive Impact Of Labor Unions," the Blackwell Firm, December 22, 2022. https://theblackwellfirm.com/the-negative-impact-of-citizens-united-and-the-positive-impact-of-labor-unions/.

David J. Craig, "How 'Citizens United' Changed Our Politics," *Columbia Magazine*, Summer 2017. https://magazine.columbia.edu/article/how-citizens-united-changed-our-politics.

Donald A. Downs, "Hillary doesn't understand the First Amendment," the *Seattle Times*, August 26, 2016. https://www.seattletimes.com/opinion/procon-should-citizens-united-be-overturned.

Karl Evers-Hillstrom, "More money, less transparency: A decade under Citizens United," OpenSecrets, January 14, 2020. https://www.opensecrets.org/news/reports/a-decade-under-citizens-united.

Terry Gross, "'Dark Money' Is Funding The 2020 Election Challenge — And Could Challenge 2024," NPR, August 5, 2021. https://www.npr.org/2021/08/05/1024741930/jane-mayer-dark-money-challenge-to-the-election-results.

Tim Lau, "Citizens United Explained," Brennan Center for Justice, December 12, 2019. https://www.brennancenter.org/our-work/research-reports/citizens-united-explained.

Stuart McPhail, "Citizens United allowed money in politics to explode. It's up to us to stop it," CREW, January 1, 2020.

https://www.citizensforethics.org/reports-investigations/crew-investigations/citizens-united-money-in-politics/.

John Pudner, "I'm a conservative against Citizens United," the *Hill,* January 20, 2020. https://thehill.com/blogs/congress-blog/politics/479049-im-a-conservative-against-citizens-united/.

David Scharfenberg, "Bernie Sanders says Citizens United has been 'disastrous.' Is he right?" the *Boston Globe*, January 16, 2020. https://www.bostonglobe.com/2020/01/16/opinion/bernie-sanders-says-citizens-united-has-been-disastrous-is-he-right/.

Noelle Shih, "The Implications of Citizens United: The Threat of Corruption in Campaign Politics in United States vs. Householder," *Columbia Undergraduate Law Review*, May 24, 2023. https://www.culawreview.org/journal/the-implications-of-citizens-united-the-threat-of-corruption-in-campaign-politics-in-united-states-vs-householder.

OPPOSING VIEWPOINTS® SERIES

Chapter 2

Should Public Servants Be Able to Use Their Positions for Financial Gain?

Chapter Preface

Show me a man that gets rich by being a politician, and I'll show you a crook," said former President Harry Truman. To view an obvious example of the corrupt behavior Truman describes, one may look to Russian President Vladimir Putin, who, according to some estimates, is one of the richest men on earth. While he draws an official salary of approximately $140,000 a year, Putin is said to be worth well in excess of $200 billion, a figure that rivals or exceeds the wealth of Elon Musk, Jeff Bezos, and other prominent moguls.

There is a name for the kind of government Putin heads, besides "dictatorship." Putin sits at the head of a vast kleptocracy, which can be defined as a government whose corrupt leaders use political power to siphon off the wealth of their people, usually by embezzling or misappropriating government funds.

Most observers have come to expect and accept this system and behavior from a man known for allegedly poisoning or defenestrating (throwing out of windows) his rivals. But the United States populace is less willing to accept that their government officials can grow wealthy while supposedly serving their constituency. Nevertheless, many of those in the political sphere in the United States are growing rich—not as rich, perhaps, as Putin, but wealthy nonetheless. In the U.S., these people are called public servants. Citizens like to say that they are working for us.

But many are also working for themselves.

It is no secret that it costs a small fortune to run for major public office in the United States of America. Many elected officials are quite wealthy even before they seek office. But many have also, like Putin, padded their wealth significantly while supposedly serving the people.

Lately, former Speaker of the House Nancy Pelosi has been the poster child for politicians whose wealth accumulates while in office. Technically, it is her husband who has made significant amounts of money by trading stocks, but Pelosi herself is certainly a beneficiary. According to the website OpenSecrets, since 2004, Pelosi's net worth has increased from $41 million to nearly $115 million. Ostensibly, nothing the Pelosis have done is illegal. Her husband owns stocks such as Apple and Microsoft, which have risen in value greatly during the period. But in her congressional position, Pelosi is privy to information about the economy and about corporations that the ordinary citizen is not. In these circumstances her husband's savvy stock trading may seem unethical at best, and perhaps even illegal, if considered insider trading. No less of a public figure than Martha Stewart served a prison sentence for the crime of saving herself a mere $45,000 through insider trading. Elected officials, however, who—allegedly—may have engaged in similar practices, have so far been exempt from repercussions.

Nancy Pelosi is not alone in accumulating vast wealth while drawing a comparatively modest salary in the hundreds of thousands of dollars. Former Senate Majority Leader Mitch McConnell's net worth has increased by tens of millions of dollars during his years of drawing a salary under $200,000. Some of that wealth has been explained away as his wife's inheritance from her mother's death, but the McConnells, like the Pelosis, have also been shrewd investors.

Other members of Congress have reputedly used inside knowledge to enhance their wealth. In 2020, just before COVID cases exploded in the U.S., several members of the United States Senate, including Richard Burr and Kelly Loeffler, sold stock just prior to the accompanying stock market crash. These legislators did so due to knowledge given to them at a closed Senate meeting. The Department of Justice subsequently investigated these transactions, but no one was ever held accountable.

Since that time, there has been a growing call in Congress to restrict its members from trading stocks altogether. Pelosi herself commented that members of Congress were still U.S. citizens, and that in a free-market economy, U.S. citizens had a right to buy and sell stock, just as anyone else. "I have great confidence in the integrity of my members," she said, in denying that anything untoward was being conducted by elected officials. Soon after, however, Pelosi bowed to public pressure and allowed the House of Representatives to move forward with legislation barring congressional stock trades. This resulted in the Ban Conflicted Trading Act, legislation "meant to prevent members of Congress from abusing their positions and profiting from public service," according to New Hampshire Democratic Congressman Chris Pappas. "Here's the simple thing," said Republican Congressman Chip Roy regarding the bill, "we don't want to be projecting to the American people that we are somehow making decisions when we are doing our job here that are connected to our own profit, our own personal financial stake." Polls revealed that over 75 percent of American voters were against lawmakers trading stocks. It is not surprising, however, that while the Ban Conflicted Trading Act bill was introduced in 2022, as of late 2023, it has not yet been voted into law.

Viewpoint 1

> *"In the case of corporate giving, it is vital for the public and all stakeholders to have confidence that philanthropy is done for legitimate purposes and not for exercising political power to gain advantage."*

Donations to Philanthropic Foundations Run by Politicians Fall into Ethical Grey Area

Archie B. Carroll

This viewpoint by Archie B. Carroll focuses on the Clinton Foundation in the leadup to Hillary Clinton's 2016 presidential candidacy. In particular, it examines donations from corporations and foreign governments to the foundation and the motivations and ethics of these donations. Carroll argues that these kinds of donations are often intended to sway political leaders into adopting policies that benefit corporations or foreign interests, effectively lobbying politicians through their donations. This kind of unofficial lobbying can have a negative impact on politics, according to Carroll, and it is particularly concerning when it is done by foreign governments. He argues that the best way to address this issue is to ban donations from foreign governments when the politician is in office or campaigning for office and to be transparent about corporate donations. Archie B. Carroll is a professor emeritus of business at the University of Georgia.

"Political CSR: why companies and foreign governments give to foundations like Clinton's," by Archie B. Carroll, February 27, 2015, https://theconversation.com/political-csr-why-companies-and-foreign-governments-give-to-foundations-like-clintons-37876. Licensed under CC BY-ND 4.0 International.

As you read, consider the following questions:

1. What are some of the reasons corporations make donations, according to Carroll?
2. What examples of corporate giving to the Clinton Foundation are mentioned in this viewpoint? What effects did these donations seemingly have?
3. What does Carroll argue is the goal of corporate social responsibility (CSR)?

Questions are being raised about the purpose and possible influence of corporate and foreign government donations to the Clinton Foundation. This is a high-profile issue now because former Secretary of State Hillary Clinton is a presumed 2016 presidential candidate.

What is the purpose of such donations? What do companies and governments expect in return when they give hundreds of millions of dollars to foundations like hers?

Philanthropy has a deep history in the relationship between business and society, and much of it is embraced by companies expecting to be thought of as good corporate citizens because of their corporate social responsibility (CSR) initiatives. One of the largest categories of CSR is philanthropic donations to foundations, charities and nonprofits.

Corporate giving has morphed, especially in Europe, into a more political activity as companies have increasingly taken on responsibilities traditionally left to governments. This is one aspect of the developing field known as political CSR. In part, it involves businesses engaging in political activity via philanthropy—often seen as lobbying—to help bring about a more beneficial business or social environment.

Enlightened Corporate Self-Interest

Companies make donations to foundations and different groups for a variety of reasons. Over the past several decades it has become evident that these donations are not made primarily out of a general sense of altruism but rather because companies expect some identifiable payoff in return. In terms of motivations for giving, companies report that most of their giving is for community investments that also help the companies and a smaller amount is categorized as "commercial," in which the companies are the primary beneficiary.

For businesses, historically, a major benefit of being socially responsible has been the enlightened self-interest argument: it is in a business's long-term self-interest to dole out shareholder earnings to charities. Philanthropy and corporate contributions in particular are a major part of this.

A more practical reason is that being socially responsible will help to ward off or shape government regulations and indirectly boost profits. In the global context, this has become a frequent practice as multinational enterprises have sought to mold the infrastructure and governance of nations in which they invest and locate.

A recent survey of 261 of the world's biggest companies showed that more than half of them increased their philanthropy in 2013 by at least 10%.

This pattern of businesses aligning their giving with expected financial benefits sought in return is now the current state of affairs among large companies.

Donations and the Bottom Line

What are the benefits to the bottom-line companies are seeking? Many answers have been given to this question, such as gaining competitive advantage, more deeply engaging customers and employees, or enhancing reputation and legitimacy with society. Some companies are simply mimicking what other large businesses are doing.

Ultimately, corporate executives and their boardroom overseers are most concerned that such donations have a positive impact on their company's profitability—or at least a benign one. They are the guardians of its financial welfare and bear ultimate responsibility to shareholders when giving away corporate resources. Increasingly, they are required to justify that CSR activities and corporate giving are consistent with the firm's strategies and financial sustainability.

Companies have traditionally tried to affect the work of government by lobbying the merits or demerits of a piece of legislation or helping get a friendly politician elected to high office. The ultimate aim is to bring about a more favorable environment in which to sell their goods and services and return more profits to their shareholders.

Making donations provides an alternate route to the same end. Though companies are reluctant to say it, it acts as an indirect method of influence. In tacit return for their beneficence, they likewise expect to create goodwill, establish or improve political connections or favors, and be able to support or defeat legislation through contributions to foundations that are important to the legislators they hope to influence.

To use a current example, this is where the Clinton Foundation—which gives money to a variety of charitable causes—enters the discussion. It's hard to pinpoint why exactly a company or foreign government is making a particular donation to a charity, such as the Clinton Foundation. But one could easily argue that a return favor is expected after a deposit is made. Recent reports have identified specific instances in which such a favor was sought—and granted.

You Scratch My Back…

The *Wall Street Journal* cited several such examples in a recent investigative report on corporate giving to the Clinton Foundation. In one reported case in 2012, the WSJ stated that Hillary Clinton lobbied the Algerian government on behalf of General Electric to pick the U.S. company to build power plants there. A month later, the foundation announced a partnership between itself and GE, along with a donation of $500,000 to $1 million. Months later GE won the contract with the Algerians.

In another 2012 case, the *WSJ* reported that Walmart pledged to donate $12 million to a public-private partnership Clinton created at the State Department and $500,000 to a charity she had helped create. One month later, during a trip to India, she lobbied against the country's ban on retail stores such as Walmart. Later, former President Clinton asked Walmart's CEO, Mike Duke, to change his schedule so he could be on a panel at the Clinton Global Initiative.

The *WSJ* reported that in some cases donations came after Mrs. Clinton helped a company and in others the donations came before she took action. Sometimes the donations came both before and after.

Foreign Governments Give with Similar Motives

Doubtless this is why foreign governments would want to make such contributions as well—to influence outcomes of elections, sway government leaders to support legislation, or to gain contracts or programs in their favor.

Why else would a foreign government make a donation to a U.S. foundation, especially one that carries a prominent name such as Clinton?

This is an especially attractive strategy as they seek to bring foreign funds back into their countries. Like lobbying, there is not always an immediate, direct quid pro quo, also like lobbying, it makes it hard for the recipients to be objective and to ignore the needs and wants of the donors. An example of this would be when a country donates to an American foundation in hopes that the company sponsoring the foundation would be more favorably disposed to building a manufacturing plant in that country.

The Clinton Foundation reportedly suspended donations from foreign governments to the foundation when she became secretary of state, but since she left her post that suspension has been lifted. Donations by foreign governments have been noticeably rising again thus putting this issue in the headlines once more.

The Ethics of Receiving Such Donations

Is it ethical to accept such donations from corporations or governments while one is running for national office or holding office? With billions of dollars at stake, the question of a real or perceived conflict of interest undoubtedly arises. And Democrats themselves have said it's not, according to the *WSJ* article.

In this case, however, it's the foreign donations that are of particular concern, since no American would accept one of their leaders being unduly influenced by another government. Foreign governments are not allowed to give money to U.S. political campaigns, making their donations to the Clinton Foundation look like a side-door way to influence the likely Democratic nominee for president.

Corporate giving, on the other hand, is easier to justify.

The quickest way to make this a non-issue would be for the Clinton Foundation to reinstate the ban immediately as long as she is politically active. And in fact the foundation has announced recently that it is reconsidering whether it should do just that.

In the case of corporate giving, it is vital for the public and all stakeholders to have confidence that philanthropy is done for legitimate purposes and not for exercising political power to gain advantage. The ethical high road requires that companies be transparent and not attempt to abuse their strong economic resources perhaps in a quest to sidestep campaign finance regulations.

CSR is primarily about improving society not augmenting business's influence. To do otherwise is to invite further government regulations, and who wants this? Certainly not the business community.

Viewpoint 2

> *"Insider trading is not a victimless crime. By throwing sand in the gears of financial markets, people trading on inside information benefit at the expense of others."*

Why Insider Trading by Lawmakers Is a Problem

Alexander Kurov and Marketa Wolfe

In this viewpoint, Alexander Kurov and Marketa Wolfe explain how there has been increased public support for banning members of Congress from trading stocks in an effort to prevent insider trading. This was encouraged by reports of senators using information from COVID-related briefings in early 2020 to inform the sale of stocks. Although there are already laws in place to prevent lawmakers from engaging in insider trading—such as the STOCK Act—many believe it does not do enough to curb it. The authors argue that insider trading has a negative impact on the economy and puts the average American at an unfair disadvantage when it comes to the stock market. Alexander Kurov is a professor of finance at West Virginia University, and Marketa Wolfe is an associate professor of economics at Skidmore College.

As you read, consider the following questions:

1. When did insider trading become illegal?

"What's insider trading and why it's a big problem," by Alexander Kurov and Marketa Wolfe, The Conversation, February 18, 2022, https://theconversation.com/whats-insider-trading-and-why-its-a-big-problem-176940. Licensed under CC BY-ND 4.0 International.

2. According to data referenced in this viewpoint, what percent of insider trading is detected?
3. According to a poll cited in this viewpoint, what percent of Americans support banning lawmakers from trading stocks?

There's a growing bipartisan push to prohibit members of Congress from buying or selling stocks. The shift follows news reports that several senators sold stocks shortly after receiving coronavirus briefings in early 2020 and that at least 57 lawmakers have failed to disclose financial transactions since 2012 as required by law.

Congress passed that law—the Stop Trading on Congressional Knowledge Act, also known as the STOCK Act—in 2012 to fight insider trading among lawmakers with increased transparency. But a chorus of legislators and governance watchdogs argue that it didn't go far enough and isn't working.

All this raises two important questions: What exactly is insider trading and what's the big deal?

We are a finance professor and an economics professor who have been studying financial markets and how investors try to take advantage of access to information for their personal gain. Our research shows it's very common but difficult to stop.

What Is Insider Trading?

Insider trading is whenever someone uses market-moving nonpublic information in the act of buying or selling a financial asset.
For example, say you work as an executive at a company that plans to make an acquisition. If it's not public, that would count as inside information. It becomes a crime if you either tell a friend about it—and that person then buys or sells a financial asset using that information—or if you make a trade yourself.

Punishment, if you're convicted for insider trading, can range from a few months to over a decade behind bars.

Insider trading became illegal in the U.S. in 1934 after Congress passed the Securities Exchange Act in the wake of the worst sustained decline in stocks in history. From Black Monday 1929 through the summer of 1932, the stock market lost 89% of its value. The act was meant to prevent a whole litany of abuses from recurring, including insider trading.

The issue was dramatized in Oliver Stone's 1987 classic movie "Wall Street," in which ruthless financier Gordon Gekko makes millions of dollars by trading on inside information on several companies obtained from his protege, Bud Fox.

"The most valuable commodity I know of is information," declares Gekko, who by the end of the film is convicted of insider trading and sent to jail.

'Informed Trading'

While insider trading typically involves trading stocks of individual companies based on information about them, it can involve any kind of information about the economy, a commodity or anything else that moves markets.

For instance, the monthly consumer price index figures have a huge impact on financial markets at the moment because of concerns about inflation and how it will affect the pace of Federal Reserve interest rate hikes. That data is collected and then closely guarded, but a small number of people have access to it before it's officially released, making the information extremely valuable if any of them wanted to profit off it.

Our own research on financial trading ahead of the release of U.S. economic data shows that financial markets tend to move in the "correct" direction in the minutes before it's released. That is, if the new data would be a positive for stocks, we saw patterns of stocks rising before that information becomes publicly available—something known as "informed trading." We also found this to be the case on data released in China and the U.K. This suggests that some traders may have advance knowledge of information in economic announcements.

Of course, alternative explanations could be that some traders are simply more skilled at collecting and analyzing available data that correctly predicts the economic announcements. For example, online prices collected in real time can be used to predict inflation levels. Also, satellite imagery and analyst forecasts can be used to predict crude oil and natural gas inventory levels.

The TRUST in Congress Act

When members of Congress trade stock while in office, they abuse the public trust—and often their positions. Legislators receive classified information to make better decisions for the health and welfare of the public. Yet, all-too-often, they leverage this insider knowledge for personal profit, or to make money for their donors.

Avoiding corruption or the appearance of corruption—and breaching the public trust—is the exact reason why we have laws like the STOCK Act in place. However, this law needs to be strengthened to correct weaknesses dealing with insider trading.

Solutions

The TRUST in Congress Act (H.R. 345) would prohibit members of Congress from trading stock while in office and require members of Congress to place their holdings in a qualified blind trust. A similar bill has also been introduced in the Senate. Congress should seize this momentum and pass into law commonsense ethics reform that will combat corruption and the appearance of corruption.

Rules for what makes a qualified blind trust are already spelled out, and require assets to be managed by an independent person instead of the beneficiary or their friends, family, or campaign.

Issue One has also strongly encouraged members of Congress to divest themselves of their publicly traded stocks and commodities when taking office, or place their assets in a diversified mutual fund.

Such measures would not only increase public confidence in the motivations behind the public officials' decisions, but also protect the public officials themselves from these accusations.

"Stopping members of Congress from trading stocks," Issue One.

Common, Profitable, and Hard to Prove

Research shows that insider trading is common and profitable, yet notoriously hard to prove and prevent. A 2020 study estimated that only about 15% of insider trading in the U.S. is detected and prosecuted.

One of the more famous—and few—examples of insider trading being prosecuted was the 2004 conviction of businesswoman and media personality Martha Stewart for selling shares based on an illegal tip from a broker. Another came in 2016, when billionaire Steven Cohen and his now-defunct SAC Capital Advisors hedge fund entered into a US$135 million settlement over insider-trading allegations. The hedge fund also paid a fine of $1.8 billion in 2014 over similar charges.

And in 2020, former U.S. Rep. Chris Collins was sentenced to 26 months in prison for passing on a confidential tip to his son and then lying about it to the FBI.

More recently, two Fed officials stepped down in September 2021 after disclosures showed they were trading extensively in 2020 at the same time the U.S. central bank was spending trillions saving the economy from the effects of the pandemic. And Sen. Richard Burr and his brother remain under investigation by the Securities and Exchange Commission over stock trades they made in February 2020 shortly after the North Carolina Republican received closed-door briefings on the pandemic.

Why It Matters

Insider trading is not a victimless crime. By throwing sand in the gears of financial markets, people trading on inside information benefit at the expense of others.

A key characteristic of well-functioning financial markets is high liquidity, which means it is easy to make large trades at low transaction costs. Insider trading adversely affects market liquidity and makes transaction costs higher, reducing investor returns. And since a lot of people have a stake in financial markets—about half of U.S. families own stocks either directly or indirectly—this behavior hurts most Americans.

Insider trading also makes it more expensive for companies to issue stocks and bonds. If investors think that insiders might be trading bonds of a company, they will demand a higher return on the bonds to compensate for their disadvantage—increasing the cost to the company. As a result, the company has less money to hire more workers or invest in a new factory.

There are also broader impacts of insider trading. It undermines public confidence in financial markets and feeds the common view that they odds are stacked in favor of the elite and against everyone else.

Furthermore, since inside traders profit from privileged access to information rather than work, this makes people believe that the system is rigged.

Curbing Insider Trading

The odds of Congress prohibiting lawmakers from trading stocks got a boost when House Speaker Nancy Pelosi recently said she may support the idea—though she'd like to see a ban also apply to the Supreme Court, which currently has no rules governing the practice. At least some Republicans, such as U.S. Rep. Kevin McCarthy and Sen. Ben Sasse, also say they support a ban.

For its part, the Fed reacted to trading by its two former officials by banning bank policymakers and senior staff from buying individual stocks or bonds.

There are also less heavy-handed ways to curb insider trading. In recent years, policymakers in the U.S. and the U.K. have tightened procedures governing the release of economic data. In the U.K., for example, dozens of public officials used to get market-moving economic data 24 hours before the public release. After the practice stopped in 2017, we found evidence of significantly less informed trading ahead of the release—suggesting it effectively prevented a lot of insider trading.

Surveys show widespread bipartisan public support for Congress to ban lawmakers from trading financial securities, with a recent poll showing 75% in favor. While that doesn't mean a law will get passed, it does put pressure on lawmakers of both parties to do something about the problem.

Viewpoint 3

> *"In a strict, bottom-line sense, Sanders has become one of those rich people against whom he has so unrelentingly railed."*

Running for President Was the Most Lucrative Thing Bernie Sanders Has Ever Done

Michael Kruse

In this excerpted viewpoint, Michael Kruse takes an in-depth look at how Bernie Sanders increased his net worth, first through real estate ventures with his wife, and then by writing best-selling books after his failed run for the Democratic nomination for president in 2016. Sanders, known for his "cheapness," nevertheless worked his way out of the middle class, becoming one of the wealthy, landowning capitalists that the avowed Democratic Socialist railed against. However, most voters, and even rival politicians, have not held his new prosperity against him. Michael Kruse is a senior staff writer at Politico *and* Politico Magazine. *He has won the National Press Foundation's Everett McKinley Dirksen Award for Distinguished Reporting of Congress, a National Headliner Award for his coverage of Donald Trump, and an honorable mention for the Toner Prize for Excellence in National Political Reporting.*

"The Secret of Bernie's Millions," by Michael Kruse, POLITICO LLC, May 24, 2019. Reprinted by permission.

As you read, consider the following questions:

1. What are some examples of Bernie Sanders' early frugality?
2. How did Sanders and his wife use real estate to increase their wealth?
3. What did Republican operative Rick Wilson mean when he called Sanders "the party apparatchik with the dacha?"

Early on in his eight years as the mayor of this city, when he typically dressed in a tieless ensemble of work boots and corduroys, Bernie Sanders one day left City Hall and found a ticket on the windshield of his rusty Volkswagen Dasher. The offense: This was the mayor's spot, and, surely, a cop had thought, this was not the mayor's car. But it was. It matched perfectly with both Sanders' image as a scrappy advocate of the little guy and his own shaky financial reality. It was the beginning of the 1980s, and he was approaching 40, a single father of a not-quite-teenage son, renting a sparse second-floor apartment and having a hard time keeping up with his bills. "Not only," he wrote on his yellow, coffee-splotched legal pads kept in archives at the University of Vermont, "do I not pay bills every month—'What, every month?'—I am unable to …" His scribbles in barely legible cursive in the margins read like reminders and afterthoughts: "gas," "light," "water."

He was, said Bruce Seifer, a friend of Sanders, an economic aide in his administration and one of many people who know him who told me this, "frugal." Seifer paused and considered the right way to put it. "That's a nice way of saying he's a cheap son of a bitch."

Today, he might still be cheap, but he's sure not poor. In the wake of his 2016 presidential run, the most lucrative thing he's ever done, the 77-year-old self-described democratic socialist is a three-home-owning millionaire with a net worth approaching at least $2 million, taking into account his publicly outlined assets and liabilities along with the real estate he owns outright. In a strict, bottom-line sense, Sanders has become one of those rich people against whom he has so unrelentingly railed. The champion of the underclass and castigator of "the 1 percent" has found himself in the socioeconomic penthouse of his rhetorical boogeymen. This development, seen mostly as the result of big bucks brought in by the slate of books he's put out in the past few years, predictably has elicited snarky pokes, partisan jabs and charges of hypocrisy. *The millionaire socialist!*

Sanders has been impatient to the point of churlish when pressed about this. "I wrote a best-selling book," he told the *New York Times* after he releasing the last 10 years of his tax returns. "If you write a best-selling book, you can be a millionaire, too." Asked on Fox News if this sort of success was "the definition of capitalism," he bristled. "You know, I have a college degree," he said.

Based on a deeper examination of his financial disclosures, tax returns, property records in Washington and Vermont, and scarcely leafed-through scraps of his financial papers housed at the University of Vermont, Sanders' current financial portrait is not only some stroke-of-luck windfall, it's also the product (with the help of his wife) of decades of planning. The upward trajectory from that jalopy of his to his relative riches now—as off-brand as it is for a man who once said he had "no great desire to be rich"—is the product of years of middle-class striving, replete with credit card debt, real estate upgrades and an array of investment funds and retirement accounts.

As an immigrant's son who started close to the bottom and has ended up near to the top, Sanders has a narrative arc that would form the backbone of the campaign story of almost any other candidate. But it's more complicated for him. There's never been anybody like Sanders in the modern political history of this country—somebody who made a career out of haranguing millionaires … and who is now a millionaire himself. There is no set strategy for how to run for president as a democratic socialist with an expensive lakefront summer house. Americans generally don't begrudge millionaires their millions—and, as Donald Trump has confirmed, the aura of wealth can serve as a useful means of self-promotion—but what to make of Sanders' apparently conflicting narratives?

"He became the very thing he criticized others for becoming and at the same time didn't *fix* any of the problems he's been railing about that got him to this point," Boston-based Democratic strategist Mary Anne Marsh told me.

"He almost at times sounds like he thinks it's inherently evil to be well-off," veteran Democratic strategist Bob Shrum said in an interview.

Does all of this make Sanders' abiding calls for economic justice more authoritative or compelling, especially as he, the ranking member on the Senate Budget Committee, argues on the 2020 hustings for costly programs like tuition-free college and universal health care, or does it defuse his drilled-home political brand and somehow muffle his message?

"I think it's only awkward if someone has sort of a facile understanding of what Bernie is trying to accomplish," senior Sanders adviser Jeff Weaver told me, "which is to give lots of people opportunities to have a modicum of security."

"It depends on how it plays out," Shrum said.

What's certain, though, is that how Sanders has become wealthy and how he has managed his money are two of the least radical things about the self-identified radical Sanders.

[...]

Looking back, the last two years of the '80s can be seen as the start of the rest of Sanders' life—because that was the time when he really started using traditional tools of the country's capitalistic financial system to put himself on firmer footing.

In May 1988, he married Jane O'Meara Driscoll, a divorced mother of three who had been his significant other the entire time he was mayor and served as the director of his administration's youth office. And that summer and fall, nearing the end of his fourth and final term at City Hall, Sanders ran for Congress as an independent, of course, and lost. But he lost by only 3.7 percentage points, and he beat the Democrat, effectively becoming, for the first time in his career, a realistic electoral option in a statewide race. "A real breakthrough for him," Nelson, the UVM professor, told me. It was a hint of what was to come.

At the time, though, that's all it was—latent potential in a moment marked by unknowns and unease. Biding time and weighing his options, Sanders scrambled for paying gigs. In January 1989, he contacted the chair of the sociology department at Hamilton College, four hours away in Clinton, New York. "I believe," Sanders wrote to Dennis Gilbert, "that I could offer your students an unusual academic perspective." After spending a semester as a fellow at the Institute of Politics at Harvard University's Kennedy School of Government, he taught classes on urban sociology and social democracy at Hamilton. Leaning on the last hunk of his salary as mayor and speeches at colleges and universities, Sanders made more than $45,000 in 1989—given inflation and the rising cost of living, it was effectively less than he had made when he was first mayor. At 50 and mulling another crapshoot of a congressional bid, he fretted. "At Hamilton," Steve Rosenfeld, his 1990 press secretary, said, "Bernie would often confide in Dennis, saying he was worried about his professional future and financial security." (Gilbert told me he doesn't recall this.)

Sanders and his wife responded by pooling resources. Central to their efforts? One of the most reliable ways that millions upon millions of Americans have sought to leverage and improve their financial fortunes: real estate.

In September 1988, according to local property records, Jane Sanders changed the house she owned on Isham Street to a house *they* owned—kicking off a spate of activity and shifting legally from "sole owner" to "Jane O'Meara Sanders and Bernard Sanders, husband and wife, as tenants by the entirety." Just two days later, they used the house to take out a mortgage of $50,000. The following February, according to a three-line recording of the transaction in the *Burlington Free Press*, Sanders sold the house he had bought in 1983 with a $49,500 mortgage for $82,000—a fine return on that first investment. Not quite three months later, leaving the more urban portion of Burlington and moving to a neighborhood closer to picturesque Lake Champlain, Bernie and Jane Sanders got a $140,000 mortgage to purchase for $175,500 a three-bedroom, two-bathroom, not-quite-1,600-square-foot house on Killarney Drive—"a red-paneled, boxy, split-level house," as Rosenfeld would describe it, "that could be in any middle-class suburb in America." Barely more than a month after that, they sold the house on Isham for $135,000.

In 1990, sometimes wearing a blue blazer missing a button and working out of a cramped basement office in the Killarney house—which had plywood tables, a painted-shut window and green indoor-outdoor carpet—and getting into hot water in the news for paying his staffers as contractors instead of as full-time employees, Sanders tried again to win Vermont's sole seat in the House—and this time, he did. In the aftermath of his victory, he was a mixture of exultant and indignant. "I'm not an insider," he said. "I know who I am. I know where I came from. I don't need to get down on my knees and ask rich people for help." After having excoriated members of Congress for voting to give themselves pay raises two years earlier—"quite beyond comprehension," he huffed in a letter to the three members of Vermont's congressional delegation that he had made public as a mayoral news release—Sanders started making considerably more than he had ever earned: $125,100 a year.

In the first half of the '90s, though—as the crotchety independent butted heads with Democrats in Washington while navigating the topsy-turvy political terrain of the time and as the election of Bill Clinton spawned the rise of increasingly virulent, Newt Gingrich-led hyperpartisanship—Sanders' prospects were far from ensured. And he used his house to hedge his bets. He signed over power of attorney to his wife, and they refinanced their home in 1991 and again in 1993, both times with mortgages larger than the one they had agreed to in 1989—$140,500 in '91, $145,600 in '93.

Sanders settled in, though, as a more and more fixed political presence in Vermont. His race in 1994 was the last one he could have lost, really, as he cemented his status and security.

In 2000, with a real estate boom underway, and with a mortgage of $62,100, he and his wife bought in essence their first second home—a condominium in Burlington, which they initially bought for Jane Sanders' elderly mother, according to Weaver, and used intermittently as a place for extended family or a rental property.

In 2004, Jane Sanders was hired as the president of Burlington College, a small, middling liberal arts school. Making a six-figure salary, she saw her tenure end in acrimony after her decision to pursue a campus expansion by making a $10 million land purchase crippled the institution. She resigned in 2014 and took with her a $200,000 severance package some called a golden parachute. In 2016, the debt-beset college closed for good, felled by "an inexperienced president," in the barbed words of Jane Sanders' successor.

In the meantime, Bernie Sanders' career was heading in the opposite direction: up. In 2006, he was elected to the Senate. At the top of a surging real estate market in 2007, with his congressional salary at $165,200, Sanders bought a row home in Washington for $489,000, adding to the condo and house on Killarney and quietly climbing some financial stair steps when far fewer people were paying him any attention.

And in 2009, when the markets were crashing and half of the 100 senators were still worth a million dollars or more, Sanders' estimated net worth clocked in at $105,000, according to the Center for Responsive Politics—at the bottom of the Senate wealth chart. In Burlington, Bernie and Jane Sanders returned to real estate, using a mortgage of $324,000 to purchase a $405,000 upgrade: a four-bedroom, 2,352-square-foot house sitting atop a slow slope of a hill up from the street on Van Patten Parkway. (They bought the house, interestingly, from her son, David Driscoll, and his wife. In 2012, for $265,000, Driscoll and his wife bought from Jane and Bernie Sanders the Killarney house. Effectively, they swapped houses. Driscoll, Weaver said, wanted to live in "his childhood home.") In 2013, Bernie and Jane Sanders refinanced the Van Patten house, taking out a mortgage of $312,275.

And in 2015, when he started running for president, he had a net worth of a little more than $700,000, according to CRP calculations, a financial picture that had all his assets in his wife's name and liabilities from a pair of mortgages as well as credit card debt listed as between $25,002 and $65,000. It made him, a spokesman said at the time, "a regular American." More "regular," perhaps, than he should have been: According to the Federal Reserve, the average household in 2015 had credit card debt of about $10,000.

"Unfortunately," Sanders said during his 2016 presidential campaign, using the same effacing opening clause and striking the same tone that he had in his financial disclosure of 40 years before, "I remain one of the poorer members of the United States Senate."

But for the politics he practiced—always—it was a useful note to sound.

He all but compared his finances to those of front-running Hillary Clinton, she of the high-dollar speaking fees. "That type of wealth," he said, "has the potential to isolate you from the reality of the world."

It wasn't long before unprecedented money for Sanders started rolling in….

[…]

Much has changed in these past four years. In 2015, Sanders had that credit card debt and two mortgages that ranged from $250,001 to $500,000, according to his Senate financial disclosure of that year. In 2016, the credit card debt was gone, and one of those mortgages had been halved. By 2018, only one of the mortgages remained; that January, records show, he paid off what was left of the $312,275 mortgage he had on his main house in Vermont.

In 2015, he published a book called *The Speech*, basically a transcript of his memorable 2010 filibuster on (what else?) corporate greed, income inequality and the decline of the middle class. Sanders made $3,035, which he donated to charity. In 2016, though, book money began to pile up. He got a $795,000 advance to write *Our Revolution*. He pocketed an additional $70,484 in royalties. In 2017, the book royalties added up to $880,091.14. And last year, while they dipped, they still were a hunk of money: $392,810.37.

The Sanders' tax returns, too, tell the tale: From 2015 to 2018, their total income went from $240,622 to $1,073,333 to $1,150,891 to $566,421. Some of that, along with money from a retirement account, according to Jane Sanders, and proceeds from a sale of a share of a family home of hers, helped pay for the lake house that I sat and looked at while listening to birds chirp in the chill of spring in the northern reaches of New England.

"Bernie is a known quantity in any socialist paradise," GOP consultant Rick Wilson told me, "the party apparatchik with the dacha ..."

This kind of characterization makes Sanders' friends and others who've known him for years all but roll their eyes.

"He's still the same cranky guy," said Terje Anderson, chairman of the Vermont Democratic Party. "I run into him at Hannaford shopping for groceries."

And in his cart, I asked, aren't the finest meats and cheeses?

"Hell no," Anderson said.

"There's no change," Niedweske added. "His priorities remain the same."

"I mean, I don't think any of Bernie's supporters said, 'Oh, well, now that he's made a lot of money selling a book ... I can't support him anymore,'" Terry Bouricius, a former Burlington city councilor and progressive who's known Sanders since the '70s, told me. "No—I don't think that happened to anybody."

A spectrum of politicos I talked to don't think this is that big of a political problem for Sanders. He has problems, they said, that are bigger than his bottom line—his persistent lack of appeal to female voters and black voters, for instance, and his generally sagging poll numbers ever since an evidently formidable Joe Biden entered the race, and the slap-in-the-face mathematical fact that this time around he's running against not Hillary Clinton but 20-plus Democrats. He is, in other words, no longer the beneficiary of the anybody-but-her voters.

"The least of his problems," Marsh, the Democratic strategist from Boston, said of Sanders' wealth.

"Detractors will needle and pester and continue to push that argument," said Joe Trippi, a Democratic strategist who's been working on presidential campaigns for almost 40 years. "But I don't think in the end it's going to have much impact."

"On the list of stuff that bothers me about Bernie," said Stuart Stevens, a GOP consultant who was the chief strategist for Mitt Romney's 2012 run, "the fact that he wrote a book and made some money doesn't bother me at all."

Ditto Democrat Bakari Sellers.

"I'm not going to sit here and shit on Bernie Sanders for being a millionaire," the former South Carolina lawmaker and current Kamala Harris supporter told me.

Why not?

"I want to be a millionaire, too!"

Viewpoint 4

> *"Both the public and the legal community believe campaign contributions influence judicial decisions. Laypersons appear to perceive little difference between an attorney lending money to a judge and contributing money to a judicial campaign."*

Campaign Contributions Can Compromise Judicial Decisions

Thomas E. McClure

In this viewpoint, Thomas E. McClure studies the relationship between contributions to judicial candidates and the perception of bias in a judge's decisions from the bench. McClure finds that even when monetary donations to a candidate do not affect decisions, there is a public perception that money has an influence. McClure's own study of judicial decisions and political donations showed mixed results, though bias in favor of those who donated large amounts of money to a judge's campaign was sometimes apparent. Thomas E. McClure is an associate professor and director of legal studies at Illinois State University. He is a founding partner of Elliott & McClure, P.C. in Kankakee County, Illinois.

Thomas E. McClure, "Perceptions of Bias: Do Campaign Contributions Create Public Perceptions of Judicial Bias?," 102 Judicature 28 (Fall/Winter 2018).

As you read, consider the following questions:

1. What is the distinction that the courts drew between an attorney's legally donating money to a judge's campaign versus donating money directly to a judge?
2. What steps did McClure take to ensure an impartial study of the judiciary and campaign contributions?
3. Why, according to McClure, might Illinois not be the best state in which to conduct his study?

In a number of cases, the Illinois Supreme Court suspended the licenses of lawyers who had loaned money directly to the trial judge who was hearing their clients' cases. They made the loans to help pay for judicial campaign expenses.[1] In each case, the court held that there was a violation of the disciplinary rule prohibiting lawyers from giving or lending "anything of value" to a judge.[2] If, however, the lawyers had disbursed the funds to the judge's campaign committee, rather than directly to the judge, the transactions would have been legal and would not have served as a basis for attorney discipline.

In another case involving attorney loans to judges, the Illinois Supreme Court addressed the disciplinary rule concerning a judge's receipt of anything of value from a lawyer:

> The general public would certainly consider it an appearance of impropriety if a judge were to accept a gift from a lawyer who has matters in the court on which that judge sits. Even if the matter were not to be heard by the judge to whom the gift is given, the public's perception would be one of suspicion, enhanced, no doubt, by the potential subliminal influence on the favored judge's colleagues.[3]

In this opinion, the court noted that the law permits a lawyer to contribute money to a judge's election campaign fund. But a judge's receipt of lawful campaign contributions from attorneys who argue before the judge can still raise questions about the judge's ability to decide cases without favoring campaign donors. I chose to focus on

Illinois trial judges in order to investigate the relationship between judicial campaign contributions and perceived impartiality because of the high number of elected lower court judges in Illinois as well as the availability of relevant data over an extended period. Indeed, the Illinois State Bar Association conducts regular polls to evaluate judges on several criteria, including impartiality. And for decades, political committees for judicial candidates have been required to report campaign contributions, and the Illinois State Board of Elections has published this information.

Mixed Results

Relationship Between Campaign Contributions and Judicial Impartiality

Empirical research offers varying perspectives on the association between judicial campaign contributions and judicial impartiality. Some scholars find no evidence of an association. For instance, Ronald Rotunda found no relationship between attorney donations and favorable majority opinions by state supreme courts in Illinois, Michigan, and Wisconsin.[4] Similarly, Margaret Williams and Corey Ditslear found little evidence suggesting that campaign contributions systematically influenced most Wisconsin Supreme Court justices—although other researchers have found evidence of potential influence among a few members of this court.[5] In a multistate supreme court study, Matias Iaryczower and Matthew Shum found an association between a justice's voting strategy and contributions made by business, unions, noncorporate lawyers, and education organizers.[6] Likewise, Eric Waltenburg and Charles Lopeman identified a transitory association between judicial contributions and case outcomes in Alabama, Kentucky, and Ohio tort decisions.[7] In a 50-state study of supreme courts, Joanna Shepherd found that contributions from pro-business groups, pro-labor groups, doctor groups, insurance companies, and lawyer groups increase the probability that justices will vote for the litigants favored by those interest groups.[8] Using the same database,

Shepherd and her colleague, Michael Kang, found that every dollar of direct contributions from pro-business groups is associated with an increase in the probability that a state supreme court justice will vote for business litigants.[9] Some scholars have found evidence of an association between contributions and judicial decisions in some states or contexts but not in others. For instance, Damon Cann discovered the existence of this association in Georgia cases.[10] However, Cann and his colleagues, Chris Bonneau and Brent Boyea, found no such relationship in the Texas Supreme Court.[11] Furthermore, in a separate study of the highest courts in Michigan, Nevada, and Texas, Bonneau and Cann found no evidence of any relationship between contributions and judicial decisions in Nevada but confirmed the existence of a quid pro quo relationship between contributions and individual justices' votes in Michigan and Texas.[12]

Campaign Contributions and the Perception of Bias

Even with these mixed research findings about the actual relationship between judicial campaign contributions and judicial impartiality, many legal observers have noted that judicial campaign contributions can nonetheless create the *perception* of improper influence.[13] Erwin Chemerinsky claimed that campaign contributions from lawyers and litigants "risk both the reality of undue influence and the appearance of impropriety."[14]

Both the public and the legal community believe campaign contributions influence judicial decisions. Laypersons appear to perceive little difference between an attorney lending money to a judge and contributing money to a judicial campaign. For example, in a January 2009 *USA Today*/Gallup poll, 52 percent of respondents considered the influence of campaign contributions on judges' rulings to be a major problem, and 89 percent said it was at least a minor problem. More than 90 percent of respondents believed a judge should be removed from a case involving a party that donated to the judge's election campaign.[15] Members of the legal community have voiced similar concerns. For example, in a

2001–02 poll of 188 state supreme court judges, 527 state appellate court judges, and 1,713 state trial judges, 26 percent of respondents said they believed campaign contributions have at least some influence on the decisions of judges; 46 percent believed campaign contributions have "just a little" influence on the decisions of judges. Only 36 percent believed that campaign contributions have no influence at all on the decisions of judges.[16] Because confidence in the judicial system depends upon the litigants' impression that their cases are decided by an impartial bench, the mere perception of impropriety creates problems for the courts.[17]

As the former executive director of Pennsylvanians for Modern Courts Shira Goodman stated:

> The truth is perception is reality when it comes to the courts. . . . We have a clear public perception problem when it comes to elected judges and the influence of campaign cash in the courtroom. But we must treat this as more than a public perception problem—it is an issue that affects the position of our courts in our governmental structure.[18]

In a 2010 study, James Gibson and Gregory Caldeira asked participants to review a series of hypothetical scenarios and assess the impartiality of a judge in the vignettes who had accepted campaign contributions. They found a moderate connection between campaign contributions and participants' perception of judicial bias. Moreover, even if a judge recused himself or herself from a case involving campaign donors, a substantial minority of participants questioned the judge's ability to be impartial.[19]

Studies of state court systems tend to focus on state supreme courts.[20] Literature on the relationship between campaign contributions and perceived judicial impartiality among trial judges is virtually nonexistent.[21] Given that attorneys and members of the public are more likely to have contact with trial courts rather than courts of review, it is important to consider perceptions of the impartiality of trial judges. This article assesses the association between the perceived impartiality of trial judges and the campaign contributions they receive from three specific populations: attorneys, interest groups, and political organizations.

Data and Methodology

Dependent Variable

The dependent variable in this study is the measure of a judge's perceived impartiality using bar poll assessments of trial judges conducted by the Illinois State Bar Association (ISBA) for circuit court judges seated in the downstate Illinois counties, as well as in the counties that border Chicago's Cook County (known as the collar counties). The ISBA does not evaluate Cook County trial judges, leaving that task to the Chicago Bar Association and the Alliance of Bar Associations for Judicial Screening, which use other methods for such assessments. In the year in which a judge faces an election, the ISBA mails confidential ballots to its members who maintain offices located in the judge's circuit. The ISBA also provides ballots, upon request, to licensed attorneys who are not ISBA members. The ISBA furnishes ballots to between one-half and three-quarters of Illinois attorneys practicing outside of Cook County. Approximately 30 percent of the attorneys return their completed ballots.[22] Before ballots are counted, attorneys must certify that they have sufficient knowledge of the judge's qualifications to allow a fair, informed opinion of the judge's qualifications. The ISBA does not count a ballot unless the attorney submits a signed statement that he or she evaluated the judicial candidate entirely on the basis of direct knowledge of a professional nature. The ISBA collects "yes" or "no" responses for several characteristics of each judge.

The impartiality rating for each circuit judge is determined by the percentage of "yes" votes cast by attorneys in response to the question: "Will the candidate [a]ct and rule impartially and free of any predisposition or improper influence?" The ISBA does not tabulate unreturned ballots and nonresponses to ballot questions. Likewise, the ISBA requires a minimum response from members of the bar before it reports the polling results. The dataset in this study includes 254 Illinois Circuit Court judges (based outside of Chicago's Cook County) who were seeking their second term of office between 1994 and 2012. In Illinois, voters elect circuit court judges in partisan elections for six-year terms. Successful candidates can run for retention in nonpartisan general elections, which require the candidate to receive 60 percent of the votes in order to be retained for another six-year term. This data does not include the small number of judges for whom the ISBA did not report bar poll scores.

The lowest rating a judge can receive is 0 percent. This occurs when all of the attorneys casting ballots answer "no" to the question as to whether the judge is impartial. Likewise, vote tabulations display the highest rating of 100 percent when all responding attorneys give a "yes" response to the impartiality question. In this study, three judges earned a 100 percent rating, and the judge receiving the lowest rating received the score of 45.41 percent. The average score was 88.3 percent, and the median was 90.5 percent.

Independent Variables

I gathered election finance information from publicly-reported campaign statements to create several independent variables. In Illinois, all political committees that receive or give contributions above a certain threshold amount must file periodic financial statements with the Illinois State Board of Elections (ISBE). Financial statements filed after 1999 are available online. The ISBE maintains physical copies of earlier statements. Campaign committees also must report a donation of $1,000 or more within five days of receipt. Every contribution from a donor exceeding $150 during a reporting period requires a disclosure of the donor's name, address, and contribution amount. Although the statements do not require the inclusion of the donor's occupation, I was able to identify attorney contributors.

I classified a donor as an attorney if one of three conditions was satisfied. First, the financial statement expressly labeled the donor as a lawyer. Second, a business donor's name matched an Illinois law firm name. Third, the donor was found through the lawyer search tool on the website of the Attorney Registration & Disciplinary Commission of the Supreme Court of Illinois. I categorized a donor as a political organization if its name identified it with a political party or candidate. I considered corporations, unions, and other organizations not expressly identified with a political party or candidate as interest groups.

The dollar amount of contributions to judges' campaign committees varied greatly. Thirty-nine judges reported no contributions from any source, whereas nine judges received in excess of $100,000 for their judicial campaigns. The largest total amount of donations reported by a single election committee was approximately $500,000. The median total contribution to each judge's campaign from all sources was $34,739. The median contribution from attorneys was $7,938. Median contributions were less than $2,000 for interest groups ($1,630) and political organizations ($1,515).

Control Variables

I included the control variables from my 2016 study of the relationship between judicial elections and the ISBA's impartiality ratings of Illinois trial judges.[23] These variables are based either on the bar poll scores or the judge's biographical data retrieved from Sullivan's Judicial Directory. The mean bar poll rating is the average ISBA poll score each judge received on the following criteria included on the bar poll: integrity, legal ability, temperament, court management, and health. I also controlled for the number of years a judge has been an attorney, gender, graduation from an Illinois public university, graduation from a top 50 law school, prior service as an elective officeholder, ISBA membership, and civic involvement (membership in a community organization open to nonlawyers). Four control variables concerned prior legal experience: career prosecutor (only prior legal experience was as a prosecutor); prosecutor; public defender but never a prosecutor;

and private practice experience. I added additional control variables that were not part of my 2016 study: "uncontested election," which indicates that a judicial candidate was unopposed in either the primary or general election, and three variables, which denote the margin of victory for the judge in the primary election, the general election, and the election with the closest margin of victory (general or primary).

Results and Discussion

When my analysis included the sole control variable of the mean bar poll rating, I found a significant association between the total amount of dollars contributed to a judicial candidate and lower impartiality ratings. Likewise, using the one-control variable model, I found that when the number of contributors giving at least $150 increased, impartiality ratings declined at a statistically significant level. The results were the same when my analyses included the broader range of control variables. There was a relationship between the number of donors giving at least $1,000 and decreased impartiality scores, but that relationship was not statistically significant when the analysis included just one control variable. Instead, the relationship became statistically significant when the full array of controls were included in the testing.

Using the single control of mean bar poll rating, there were significant associations between attorney donations and impartiality ratings. The total amount of dollars contributed to a judicial candidate by attorneys, the number of attorneys donating at least $150, and the number of attorneys donating at least $1,000 were associated with lower impartiality ratings at a significant level. The results were virtually the same when I included all of the control variables.

The relationship between total donations made by interest groups and lower judicial impartiality was not at a statistically significant level, regardless of whether the mean bar poll rating was the sole control variable or all of the variables served as controls.

Nor was the association between political organization total contributions and lower integrity ratings statistically significant under either analysis.

In sum, this study demonstrates the existence of the hypothesized relationship between lower impartiality scores and judicial contributions in general as well as for attorney contributions. However, there was no statistically significant association as to decreased impartiality scores with campaign donations made by either interest groups or political organizations. The absence of this correlation is not completely surprising given the lower amounts contributed to trial judges by these groups.

Concluding Comments

A limitation of this study's analysis is that the data came from a single state, Illinois, which has experienced high-profile instances of political corruption. Indeed, as of early 2013, four of the state's seven most recent governors had been imprisoned.[24] Illinois also has fared poorly in state rankings of federal corruption convictions for public officials per capita (6th most) and in Oguzhan Dincer and Michael Johnston's survey of state political reporters regarding perceived legal and illegal corruption (2nd highest).[25] On the other hand, a study by Damon Cann and Jeff Yates concerning the perception of state high courts ranked Illinois in the middle of the pack in terms of legitimacy (23 out of 50).[26] Thus, it is unclear to what extent the results of this study of Illinois judges can be generalized and applied to the judiciaries of other states. A $10,000 contribution to a judicial campaign in Illinois may be more likely to create a perception of bias because the state already has earned a reputation for corruption. Alternatively, a $10,000 contribution might be more likely to generate the appearance of impropriety in a state in which public officials are presumably ethical because expectations are higher. Indeed, the implications of judicial bias may be more scandalous for a candidate with a moral reputation than a candidate who is already considered unethical. More research is thus needed to determine the extent to which judicial campaign contributions correlate with perceptions of judicial bias in states with a different political culture.

Additional research could also include a dependent variable that permits more nuance in perceptions of impartiality. The ISBA bar poll limits an attorney to "yes" or "no" responses to the inquiry about the judicial candidate's impartiality. This choice forces attorneys to dichotomize their likely nondichotomous perceptions of a judge's impartiality. This lack of gradation should be expected to attenuate the association between campaign contributions and perceptions of judicial impartiality. Indeed, attorneys who perceive a judge as being moderately impartial are forced to rate these judges either the same as judges whom they believe to be extremely biased or the same as judges perceived to be unquestionably impartial. Poll options that capture more shades of distinction, such as a 0–10 scale, would better permit researchers to estimate the association between campaign contributions and perceptions of judicial impartiality.

The final, and perhaps most important, avenue for future research would be to test for a causal relationship underlying the negative association between perceptions of a judge's impartiality and the campaign contributions the judge has received. The nature of my research design does not support causal claims. Nevertheless, the results are consistent with at least two possible causal relationships. Initially, judges with lower levels of perceived impartiality may be more likely to receive campaign contributions than judges with higher levels of perceived impartiality. In this situation, donors would expect that their contributions would influence these lower-impartiality judges.

Alternatively, a judge's receipt of campaign contributions could lower attorney perceptions of the judge's impartiality. This is especially likely if attorneys learn through courtroom gossip or other avenues about contributions made to a judge's campaign. Although both of these options have normative implications, the possibility that campaign contributions influence the perception of judicial impartiality has implications for the institutional legitimacy of the courts. In this interpretation, the results strengthen concerns raised by research conducted by Gibson and Caldeira establishing a causal connection between acceptance of campaign contributions and judicial legitimacy and impartiality.

The citizenry's perceptions of the legitimacy of the judiciary and its actors are critical to the viability of an effective legal system.[27] Public confidence in the courts strongly correlates with perceptions that the courts are fair and that judges are fair.[28] Federalist 78 notes that the judiciary has "neither FORCE nor WILL, but merely judgment."[29]

The results of this study add correlational data to the literature about whether campaign contributions influence a jurist's judgments.

Footnotes

1. *See, e.g.*, *In re Lane*, 535 N.E.2d 866 (Ill. 1989) (suspending lawyer for one year for contributions to judge); *In re Lidov*, 544 N.E.2d 294 (Ill. 1989) (suspending lawyer for six months for contributions to judge); *In re Chatz*, 546 N.E.2d 613 (Ill. 1989) (suspending lawyer for one year for contributions to judge).
2. Ill. Rev. Stat. 1989, ch. 110A, §7-110(a), *amended by* 735 Ill. Comp. Stat. 2010, §8.4(f).
3. *In re Corboy*, 528 N.E.2d 694, 701 (Ill. 1988).
4. Ronald D. Rotunda, *Judicial Impartiality and Judicial Campaign Contributions: Evaluating the Data*, 5 Engage: J. Federalist Soc'y's Prac. Group 122, 124–26 (2004).
5. Margaret S. Williams & Corey A. Ditslear, Bidding for Justice: The Influence of Attorneys' Contributions on State Supreme Courts, 28 Just. Sys. J. 135, 152–53 (2007).
6. Matias Iaryczower & Matthew Shum, Money in Judicial Politics: Individual Contributions and Collective Decisions, 25 (Oct. 3, 2013) (unpublished manuscript) (on file with Department of Politics, Princeton University).
7. Eric Waltenburg & Charles Lopeman, *Tort Decisions and Campaign Dollars*, 28 Pol. & Pol'y. 241, 242 (2000).
8. Joanna M. Shepherd, *Money, Politics, and Impartial Justice*, 58 Duke L.J. 623, 628–30 (2009).
9. Michael S. Kang & Joanna M. Shepherd, *The Partisan Price of Justice: An Empirical Analysis of Campaign Contributions and Judicial Decisions*, 86 N.Y.U. L. Rev. 69, 73 (2011).
10. Damon M. Cann, *Justice for Sale? Campaign Contributions and Judicial Decisionmaking*, 7 St. Pol. & Pol'y Q. 281, 292 (2007).
11. Damon M. Cann et al., *Campaign Contributions and Judicial Decisions in Partisan and Nonpartisan Elections, in*New Directions in Judicial Politics 38 (Kevin T. McGuire ed., 2012).

12. Chris W. Bonneau & Damon M. Cann, *The Effect of Campaign Contributions on Judicial Decisionmaking* 19 (Feb. 4, 2009) (unpublished manuscript).
13. *See, e.g.*, Kenneth J. Aulet, *It's Not Who Hires You but Who Can Fire You: The Case Against Retention Elections*, 44 Colum. J. L. & Soc. Probs. 589, 600 (2011) (citing *Republican Party of Minn. v. White*, 536 U.S. 765, 790 (2002) (O'Connor, J., concurring)); Stuart Banner, Note, *Disqualifying Elected Judges from Cases Involving Campaign Contributors*, 40 Stan. L. Rev. 449, 465–66 (1988); Donald W. Jackson & James W. Riddlesperger, Jr., *Money and Politics in Judicial Elections: The 1988 Election of the Chief Justice of the Texas Supreme Court*, 74 Judicature 184, 189 (1991); Marlene Nicholson & Bradley Scott Weiss, *Funding Judicial Campaigns in the Circuit Court of Cook County*, 70 Judicature 17, 25 (1986); Thomas M. Susman, *Reciprocity, Denial, and the Appearance of Impropriety: Why Self-Recusal Cannot Remedy the Influence of Campaign Contributions on Judges' Decisions*, 26 J. L. & Pol. 359, 363–65 (2011); Stephen J. Ware, *Judicial Elections, Judicial Impartiality and Legitimate Judicial Lawmaking:*WilliamsYulee v. The Florida Bar, 68 Vand. L. Rev. En Banc 59, 70 (2015).
14. Erwin Chemerinsky, *Preserving an Independent Judiciary: The Need for Contribution and Expenditure Limits in Judicial Elections*, 74 Chi.-Kent L. Rev. 133, 134 (1998).
15. Joan Biskupic, *Supreme Court Case with the Feel of a Best Seller*, USA Today (Feb. 16, 2009, 10:12 P.M.), http://usatoday30.usatoday.com/news/washington/2009-02-16-grishamcourt_N.htm.
16. Greenberg Quinlan Rosner Research, Inc., Justice at Stake – State Judges Frequency Questionnaire, http://www.justiceatstake.org/media/cms/JASJudgesSurveyResults_EA8838C0504A5.pdf (last visited May 25, 2018).
17. Sara C. Benesh, *Understanding Public Confidence in American Courts*, 68 J. Pol. 697, 703–04 (2006); Cann, *supra*note 10, at 282; Roy A. Schotland, *Elective Judges' Campaign Financing: Are State Judges' Robes the Emperor's Clothes of American Democracy?*, 2 J. L. & Pol. 57, 90 (1985).
18. Shira J. Goodman, *The Danger Inherent in the Public Perception that Justice is for Sale*, 60 Drake L. Rev. 807, 818 (2012).
19. James L. Gibson & Gregory Caldeira, *Judicial Impartiality, Campaign Contributions, and Recusals: Results from a National Survey*, 10 J. Empirical Legal Stud. 76, 85 (2013).
20. Damon M. Cann & Jeff Yates, These Estimable Courts: Understanding Public Perceptions of State Judicial Institutions and Legal Policy-Making 23 (2016).
21. *But see* Thomas E. McClure, *Do Contributions to Judicial Campaigns Create the Appearance of Corruption?*, in Corruption, Accountability and Discretion 85 (Nancy Lind & Cara Rabe-Hemp eds., 2017) (discussing the association between perception of integrity and campaign contributions for Illinois trial judges).
22. Thomas E. McClure, *Do Judicial Elections Impact the Perception of Impartiality? A Comparison of Bar Poll Ratings of Elected and Appointed Illinois Downstate and Collar County Trial Judges*, 37 Just. Sys. J. 157, 160 n.8 (2016).
23. *Id.* at 162–64.
24. *4 of Illinois' Last 7 Governors Went to Prison*, Daily Herald (Jan. 29, 2013, 7:48 P.M.), http://www.dailyherald.com/article/20130129/news/701299665.
25. Harry Enten, *Ranking the States from Most to Least Corrupt*, FiveThirtyEight (Jan. 23, 2015, 7:00 A.M.), https://fivethirtyeight.com/features/ranking-the-states-from-most-to-least-corrupt; Oguzhan C. Dincer & Michael Johnston, *Measuring Illegal and Legal*

Corruption in American States: Some Results from the Corruption in America Survey, Edmond J. Safra Ctr. Ethics (Dec. 1, 2014), https://ethics.harvard.edu/blog/measuring-illegal-and-legal-corruption-american-states-some-results-safra.

26. Cann & Yates, *supra* note 20, at 28–29.
27. *Id.* at 24.
28. Benesh, *supra* note 17, at 703–04.
29. The Federalist No. 78, at 463–471 (Alexander Hamilton) (Clinton Rossiter ed., 2003).

Periodical and Internet Sources Bibliography

The following articles have been selected to supplement the diverse views presented in this chapter.

Noah Bookbinder and Dennis Aftergut, "Opinion: Supreme Court Justice Clarence Thomas' corruption is intolerable. Here's what we can do about It," *Los Angeles Times*, August 10, 2023. https://www.latimes.com/opinion/story/2023-08-10/supreme-court-justice-clarence-thomas-corruption-gifts-propublica-ethics-congress.

Emma Camp, "Judges Who Sent Kids to Detention Centers for Financial Kickbacks Ordered to Pay Over $200 Million," *Reason*, August 8, 2022. https://reason.com/2022/08/18/judges-who-sent-kids-to-detention-centers-for-financial-kickbacks-ordered-to-pay-over-200-million/.

Vance Cariaga, "Grant Cardone Asks How Politicians That Make $100k Suddenly Become Multimillionaires — Here's the Harsh Reality," *Yahoo Finance*, September 11, 2023. https://finance.yahoo.com/news/grant-cardone-asks-politicians-100k-144919056.html.

Rachel Curry, "Can elected officials own and trade stocks?," *Public*. https://public.com/learn/can-elected-officials-own-and-trade-stocks.

The Editorial Board, "Why Is George Santos Still in Office?," the *New York Times*, May 19, 2023. https://www.nytimes.com/2023/05/19/opinion/george-santos-expulsion.html.

Meghan Faulkner and Robert Maguire, "Clarence Thomas's decisions have been benefiting wealthy donors like Harlan Crow—for decades," *CREW*, May 1, 2023. https://www.citizensforethics.org/news/analysis/clarence-thomass-decisions-have-been-benefiting-wealthy-donors-like-harlan-crow-for-decades/.

Sue Fothergill, "No one asked for a pro-corruption Congress," *Fulcrum*, January 12, 2023. https://thefulcrum.us/corruption-in-congress.

Dylan Hedtler-Gaudette and Walter M. Shaub, Jr., "American Voters Say Corruption is a Concern; Congress Should Heed the Message," *POGO*, November 8, 2021. https://www.pogo.org/analysis/2021/11/american-voters-say-corruption-is-a-concern-congress-should-heed-the-message.

Robert Lee, "Elected officials shouldn't enrich themselves while serving," May 25, 2020, the *Ada News*. https://www.theadanews.com/opinion/columns/elected-officials-shouldnt-enrich-themselves-while-serving/article_ba9ae866-54ab-507c-b498-9fe21181d46a.html.

Erika Sanders, "Members of Congress Shouldn't Trade Stocks, But Even in Solutions Loopholes Remain," Just Security, February 2, 2023. https://www.justsecurity.org/84988/members-of-congress-shouldnt-trade-stocks-but-even-in-solutions-loopholes-remain/.

David Sirota, "Blame the US supreme court for the Bob Menendez scandal," the *Guardian*, September 25, 2023. https://www.theguardian.com/commentisfree/2023/sep/25/menendez-scandal-supreme-court-corruption.

Rich Tenorio, "Filthy Rich Politicians: Journalist Matt K Lewis on Trump, ethics and money in Washington," the *Guardian*, July 22, 2023. https://www.theguardian.com/books/2023/jul/22/filthy-rich-politicians-matt-k-lewis-congress-book.

OPPOSING VIEWPOINTS® SERIES

CHAPTER 3

Has Dishonesty from Politicians Gone Too Far?

Chapter Preface

It speaks to American values that one of the country's founding stories concerns a president's truth telling. For generations children were told the tale of how America's first president, George Washington, cut down a cherry tree. When confronted by his angry father, Washington overcame his fear of punishment and confessed, saying: "Father, I cannot tell a lie." The persistence of the legend demonstrates how avidly Americans desire forthright leaders.

Unfortunately, the story itself is a complete fabrication, the invention of one of Washington's first biographers, an itinerant minister and bookseller named Mason Locke Weems. Weems wanted to give the American public the portrait of a man whose "unparalleled rise and elevation were due to his Great Virtues." According to the website run by "George Washington's Mount Vernon," Weems "wanted to present Washington as the perfect role model, especially for young Americans." He not only accomplished this, but made a good sum of money mixing into his biography what we now recognize as myths about America's first war hero and president. The cherry tree story did not even appear in the first edition of Weems' biography of Washington. It was not until the fifth edition of the book was released in 1806 that the cherry tree legend entered the American consciousness. "When the legend becomes fact, print the legend" runs the famous line from director John Ford's film *The Man Who Shot Liberty Valance*.

The story seems like a quaint tale in light of recent presidential history. "Every president lies—at some point," Glenn Kessler, Salvador Rizzo, and Meg Kelly state matter-of-factly in their book, *Donald Trump and His Assault on Truth*. Most American citizens know the recent history of presidential untruthfulness: George Bush's famous declaration, "Read my lips: no new taxes," that preceded his hiking of taxes; Bill Clinton's looking directly at the camera while stating he did not have sexual relations with Monica Lewinsky; George W. Bush's garnering of support for the

2003 invasion of Iraq by falsely telling the world that Saddam Hussein was stockpiling "weapons of mass destruction"; and Barack Obama's oft-repeated promise in 2013 that "if you like your health care plan, you can keep it" even though The Affordable Care Act (ACA), alternatively known as "Obamacare," had no such provision.

But none of these presidential untruths prepared Americans for the endless barrage of lies, prevarications, misstatements, deceptions, deceits, dishonesties, and misrepresentations proclaimed by the nation's 45th president, Donald J. Trump.

In their book, *Donald Trump and the Assault on Truth*, the authors discuss their role as members of the *Washington Post*'s fact checker staff. Their job was literally to catalogue "every false or misleading statement he made." Three years into Trump's presidency, on January 20, 2020, their count stood at 16,241. And that was not even including Trump's tempestuous—and mendacious—final year in the White House, when he concocted the biggest whopper of them all, the completely dishonest and perfidious assertion that he had won the November 2020 election "by a lot," as he grew used to saying.

Trump's successor, President Joe Biden, has restored some measure of dignity to the Oval Office, but he, too, is prone to twisting the truth. The *Federalist*, a conservative website, claims Biden has told 252 lies in his first two-and-a-half years in office. By contrast, the *Washington Post* reported that Donald Trump on September 7, 2018, alone "made 125 [false or misleading] claims."

Trump has never backed down from "the big lie" about election fraud, as his detractors began to call it, and among his followers—after all, 74 million people voted for him in 2020—many have taken his words as truth. Trump's deceits have led to a fracturing of the truth as we know it in politics. Many failed politicians around the country—and the world—have followed his lead and claimed election fraud after a losing campaign. In Brazil, for example, former President Jair Bolsonaro, a self-proclaimed Trump wannabe, also alleged fraud even before he lost his bid for re-election. He has been held accountable for his lies and is currently on trial in a Brazilian court of law.

Sometimes such claims reach ludicrous proportions. Kandiss Taylor lost Georgia's Republican gubernatorial primary to incumbent Brian Kemp but refused to concede and claimed election fraud, for which she offered no proof. Kemp garnered 74 percent of the primary vote. And Taylor? She received 3.4 percent.

Many commentators have observed that we are now living in a "post truth" political world, where, according to the European Center for Populism Studies, "debate is framed largely by appeals to emotion disconnected from the details of policy, and by the repeated assertion of talking points to which factual rebuttals are ignored." In this post-factual society, fake news, propaganda, and fallacious arguments rule the day, and truth and logic are the losers. The implications are dire for democracy. America has been led down a long and dangerous path since the days of "Father, I cannot tell a lie."

Viewpoint 1

> *"Leaders who lose their way are not necessarily bad people; rather, they lose their moral bearings, often yielding to seductions in their paths. Very few people go into leadership roles to cheat or do evil, yet we all have the capacity for actions we deeply regret unless we stay grounded."*

Leaders Often Ethically Lose Their Way

Bill George

In this viewpoint, Bill George examines how and why those in leadership positions ethically lose their way. While he believes that money, fame, and power are not necessarily bad reasons for becoming a leader, he also states that there must be an inner satisfaction with achieving success. Those who lose their way often disregard the advice of others, only listening to what they want to hear. Leaders who reach this stage are prone to make big mistakes, George believes. For George, the solution to this problem is for leaders to surround themselves with good people who will tell them the truth—and then listen to these people. Bill George is an American businessman and academic. He is a professor of management practice, and a Henry B. Arthur Fellow of Ethics at Harvard Business School. He previously served as chairman and chief executive officer of Medtronic.

"Why Leaders Lose Their Way," by Bill George, Harvard Business College Working Knowledge, June 6, 2011. Reprinted by permission.

As you read, consider the following questions:

1. What are some examples George cites of leaders who have gone astray?
2. What is an imposter complex?
3. What are some ways those in power can avoid the pitfalls that accompany egotistical and self-centered leadership?

In recent months several high-level leaders have mysteriously lost their way. Dominique Strauss-Kahn, former head of the International Monetary Fund and a leading French politician, was arraigned on charges of sexual assault. Before that David Sokol, rumored to be Warren Buffett's successor, was forced to resign for trading in Lubrizol stock prior to recommending that Berkshire Hathaway purchase the company. Examples abound of other recent failures:

- Hewlett-Packard CEO Mark Hurd resigned for submitting false expense reports concerning his relationship with a contractor.
- U.S. Senator John Ensign (R-NV) resigned after covering up an extramarital affair with monetary payoffs.
- Lee B. Farkas, former chairman of giant mortgage lender Taylor, Bean & Whitaker, in April was found guilty for his role in one of the largest bank fraud schemes in American history.

These talented leaders were highly successful in their respective fields and at the peak of their careers. This makes their behavior especially perplexing, raising questions about what caused them to lose their way:

- Why do leaders known for integrity and leadership engage in unethical activities?
- Why do they risk great careers and unblemished reputations for such ephemeral gains?
- Do they think they won't get caught or believe their elevated status puts them above the law?

- Was this the first time they did something inappropriate, or have they been on the slippery slope for years?

In these ongoing revelations, the media, politicians, and the general public frequently characterize these leaders as bad people, even calling them evil. Simplistic notions of good and bad only cloud our understanding of why good leaders lose their way, and how this could happen to any of us.

Leaders who lose their way are not necessarily bad people; rather, they lose their moral bearings, often yielding to seductions in their paths. Very few people go into leadership roles to cheat or do evil, yet we all have the capacity for actions we deeply regret unless we stay grounded.

Self-Reflection: A Path to Leadership Development

Before anyone takes on a leadership role, they should ask themselves, "Why do I want to lead?" and "What's the purpose of my leadership?" These questions are simple to ask, but finding the real answers may take decades. If the honest answers are power, prestige, and money, leaders are at risk of relying on external gratification for fulfillment. There is nothing wrong with desiring these outward symbols as long as they are combined with a deeper desire to serve something greater than oneself.

Leaders whose goal is the quest for power over others, unlimited wealth, or the fame that comes with success tend to look to others to gain satisfaction, and often appear self-centered and egotistical. They start to believe their own press. As leaders of institutions, they eventually believe the institution cannot succeed without them.

The Leadership Trap

While most people value fair compensation for their accomplishments, few leaders start out seeking only money, power, and prestige. Along the way, the rewards—bonus checks, newspaper articles, perks, and stock appreciation—fuel increasing desires for more.

This creates a deep desire to keep it going, often driven by desires to overcome narcissistic wounds from childhood. Many times, this desire is so strong that leaders breach the ethical standards

Partisan Differences in Ethical Priorities

What's more valuable to you: agency or communion? In *Social Psychology Quarterly*, Kimmo Eriksson considers whether Democrats and Republicans answer this question differently. He asks, first, which political parties are more likely to consider agency (self-oriented motivation) and communion (other-oriented motivation) as more valuable to society? Second, do Democrats and Republicans rate their own party's members as more likely to embody the traits they find more important? And third, do these politicians value human nature or human uniqueness?

Eriksson finds that a large majority of Democrats value communion over agency. Among the Republicans, the opposite was true. He also found evidence of ingroup bias. Respondents were asked to evaluate the "average" Democrat or Republican in comparison to the "average American." Democrats rated other Democrats as more likely to show communal orientations, while Republicans rated other Republicans as more likely to be agentic. However, neither Democrats nor Republicans showed this ingroup bias toward themselves: respondents from both parties rated themselves more agentic than communal.

This study also investigated perceptions of humanization among Republicans and Democrats. Associated literature says that liberals should emphasize human nature (differentiating humans from machines) while conservatives should emphasize human uniqueness (differentiating humans from animals). Based on these values, liberal Democrats and conservative Republicans should "dehumanize" each other in the areas they value most. Eriksson's results, however, do not support that perspective. Instead, he asserts that orientations toward agency and communion give us the best insight into American political behavior.

"Politicians: selfish or selfless?," by Simone N. Durham, American Sociological Association, January 11, 2019.

that previously governed their conduct, which can be bizarre and even illegal.

As Novartis chairman Daniel Vasella (HBS PMD 57) told *Fortune* magazine, "for many of us the idea of being a successful manager—leading the company from peak to peak, delivering the goods quarter by quarter—is an intoxicating one. It is a pattern of celebration leading to belief, leading to distortion. When you achieve good results… you are typically celebrated, and you begin to believe that the figure at the center of all that champagne-toasting is yourself."

When leaders focus on external gratification instead of inner satisfaction, they lose their grounding. Often they reject the honest critic who speaks truth to power. Instead, they surround themselves with sycophants who tell them what they want to hear. Over time, they are unable to engage in honest dialogue; others learn not to confront them with reality.

The Dark Side of Leadership

Many leaders get to the top by imposing their will on others, even destroying people standing in their way. When they reach the top, they may be paranoid that others are trying to knock them off their pedestal. Sometimes they develop an impostor complex, caused by deep insecurities that they aren't good enough and may be unmasked.

To prove they aren't impostors, they drive so hard for perfection that they are incapable of acknowledging their failures. When confronted by them, they convince themselves and others that these problems are neither their fault nor their responsibility. Or they look for scapegoats to blame for their problems. Using their power, charisma, and communications skills, they force people to accept these distortions, causing entire organizations to lose touch with reality.

At this stage leaders are vulnerable to making big mistakes, such as violating the law or putting their organizations' existence at risk. Their distortions convince them they are doing nothing wrong, or they rationalize that their deviations are acceptable to achieve a greater good.

During the financial crisis, Lehman CEO Richard Fuld refused to recognize that Lehman was undercapitalized. His denial turned balance sheet misjudgments into catastrophe for the entire financial system. Fuld persistently rejected advice to seek added capital, deluding himself into thinking the federal government would bail him out. When the crisis hit, he had run out of options other than bankruptcy.

It's lonely at the top, because leaders know they are ultimately responsible for the lives and fortunes of people. If they fail, many get deeply hurt. They often deny the burdens and loneliness, becoming incapable of facing reality. They shut down their inner voice, because it is too painful to confront or even acknowledge; it may, however, appear in their dreams as they try to resolve conflicts rustling around inside their heads.

Meanwhile, their work lives and personal lives get out of balance. They lose touch with those closest to them—their spouses, children, and best friends—or co-opt them with their points of view. Eventually, they lose their capacity to think logically about important issues.

Values-Centered Leadership

Leading is high stress work. There is no way to avoid the constant challenges of being responsible for people, organizations, outcomes, and uncertainties in the environment. Leaders who move up have greater freedom to control their destinies, but also experience increased pressure and seduction.

Leaders can avoid these pitfalls by devoting themselves to personal development that cultivates their inner compass, or True North. This requires reframing their leadership from being heroes to being servants of the people they lead. This process requires thought and introspection because many people get into leadership roles in response to their ego needs. It enables them to transition from seeking external gratification to finding internal satisfaction by making meaningful contributions through their leadership.

Maintaining their equilibrium amid this stress requires discipline. Some people practice meditation or yoga to relieve stress, while others find solace in prayer or taking long runs or walks. Still others find relief through laughter, music, television, sporting events, and reading. Their choices don't matter, as long as they relieve stress and enable them to think clearly about work and personal issues.

A System to Support Values-Centered Leadership

The reality is that people cannot stay grounded by themselves. Leaders depend on people closest to them to stay centered. They should seek out people who influence them in profound ways and stay connected to them. Often their spouse or partner knows them best. They aren't impressed by titles, prestige, or wealth accumulation; instead, they worry that these outward symbols may be causing the loss of authenticity.

Spouses and partners can't carry this entire burden though. We need mentors to advise us when facing difficult decisions. Reliable mentors are entirely honest and straight with us, defining reality and developing action plans.

In addition, intimate support groups like the True North Groups, with whom people can share their life experiences, hopes, fears, and challenges, are invaluable. Members of our True North Group aren't impressed by external success, but care enough about us as human beings and as leaders to confront us when we aren't being honest with ourselves.

As Senator Ensign told his fellow senators in a farewell speech in May, "When one takes a position of leadership, there is a very real danger of getting caught up in the hype surrounding that status … Surround yourselves with people who will be honest with you about how you really are and what you are becoming, and then make them promise to not hold back… from telling you the truth."

Viewpoint 2

> *"When we asked respondents to 'imagine that a future prime minister has to choose between acting honestly and delivering the policy that most people want,' 71% chose honesty and only 16% delivery."*

Voters Prize Honesty Above All Else in Their Leaders

Alan Renwick

In this viewpoint, Alan Renwick examines how and why the integrity of leaders is a highly prized trait. The vast majority of voters expect leaders to be honest and follow the rules. The people surveyed in the study Renwick cites did not want power to be concentrated in the hands of the few, because constituents don't trust politicians, and especially don't trust politicians closest to power. Renwick concludes by issuing something of a warning to politicians: leaders who violate the principles of honesty and integrity harm themselves and damage confidence in democracy. Alan Renwick is a professor of democratic politics at University College London (UCL). He formerly worked at the Universities of Oxford and Reading, obtaining a PhD on processes of institutional design in Hungary, Czechoslovakia, and Poland during the transition from communism.

"Voters value honesty in their politicians above all else – new study," by Alan Renwick, The Conversation, January 26, 2022. https://theconversation.com/voters-value-honesty-in-their-politicians-above-all-else-new-study-175589. Licensed under CC-BY-ND 4.0 International.

As you read, consider the following questions:

1. Besides honesty, what are some of the other leadership traits voters value?
2. How do those surveyed feel about the role of civil servants?
3. What does the survey indicate about how power should be distributed in the UK?

As pressure mounts on the UK prime minister, Boris Johnson, members of his party are considering their options. Should they topple him or keep him? Those who want him out fear that the public will not forgive the string of alleged social events held in Downing Street while the rest of the country lived under strict COVID lockdowns. Their anger may cost the Conservatives dearly at the next election. Those who are hesitating do so because Johnson had been such an electoral success story before this scandal.

We at the UCL Constitution Unit are conducting a major study of public attitudes to democracy in the UK that sheds new light on what matters most to voters. Our latest findings from a large-scale survey of the UK population conducted last summer suggest Conservative MPs are right to be concerned about the fallout of "partygate." Integrity is extremely important to voters. It is in fact valued above all other traits in a politician.

When we asked about a range of characteristics that politicians should have, "being honest" came top. This was followed by "owning up when they make mistakes." "Getting things done" and "being inspiring" were far behind.

Johnson has a trademark tactic—seen repeatedly at Prime Minister's Questions—of batting away critics by saying he is focused on delivering the people's priorities. When asked about any potentially questionable behaviour or incidents, he insists that members of the public care more about "getting Brexit done" than it does about anything else.

However, our findings suggest otherwise. When we asked respondents to "imagine that a future prime minister has to choose between acting honestly and delivering the policy that most people want," 71% chose honesty and only 16% delivery. When we asked whether respondents agreed more that "healthy democracy requires that politicians always act within the rules" or that "healthy democracy means getting things done, even if that sometimes requires politicians to break the rules," 75% chose the former and just 6% the latter.

It is worth repeating that these findings come from the summer—before the Owen Paterson affair and "partygate." They are not knee-jerk reactions to short-term headlines. The vast majority of voters expect politicians to act honestly and follow the rules.

Limiting Power at the Very Top

Another less obvious but equally important pattern emerged from our findings. Voters do not want power to be unduly concentrated in the hands of the prime minister and their government. Many favour at least somewhat greater powers for parliament—45% think MPs should decide what the House of Commons debates, against 30% who think the prime minister or government should do so.

Even more clearly, and perhaps surprisingly, most want judges to constrain ministers too. We asked respondents to "imagine there is a dispute over whether the government has the legal authority to decide a particular matter on its own or whether it needs parliament's approval," and to consider how the dispute should be settled. Most (51%) said it should be settled by judges and only 27% chose government ministers or politicians in parliament. We also asked about whether judges should play a role in resolving whether a new law violates rights. Depending on the rights that we asked about, between 65% and 77% of respondents said that the courts should have their current powers under the Human Rights Act or even be given stronger powers to strike down laws directly.

A large majority also said that civil servants should be "neutral and permanent government employees" rather than "appointed by the government of the day." And most respondents thought that someone who had previously said the BBC should be neutral in its reporting could be a suitable candidate for BBC chair, but that someone who had said the BBC should be less critical of government could not.

The reason for these answers appears clear: most people don't trust politicians, and they trust the politicians closest to power least. They therefore welcome limits on what those in power can do.

Our study is investigating public attitudes to democracy not only through surveys, but also through a citizens' assembly, which shows whether people think the same or differently once they have thought and learnt about the issues in depth. We will publish full results of the Citizens' Assembly on Democracy in the UK in the spring. But initial findings fit the survey responses closely. Assembly members said "we feel dissatisfied with how democracy is working in the UK today because there is a lack of honesty and integrity in politics." By large majorities, they favoured greater powers for parliament and the courts vis-à-vis the executive.

However the current ructions in the Conservative Party pan out in the coming weeks, those in power should be clear: people in the UK expect their leaders to act with integrity—and they expect a system of checks and balances on executive power to be maintained. A leader who violates these principles harms him or herself and damages confidence in democracy.

Viewpoint 3

> *"A recent study of presidential deception found that all American presidents—from Washington to Trump - have told lies, and knowingly so, in their public statements. The most effective of presidents have sometimes been effective precisely because they were skilled at manipulation and deception."*

All Presidents Lie, but How and Why They Lie Determines Their Reputation

Michael Blake

In this viewpoint, Michael Blake asserts that while all presidents tell untruths, what separates them is the rationale behind their falsehoods: when and for what purpose do they deceive? Blake states that the most successful presidents have sometimes been effective due to their skill in deception. Presidents who lie for vanity or self-interest are likely to lose public approval, but those who deceive for the public good may well be celebrated. Blake takes a philosophical view of lying, suggesting that telling falsehoods may not always be immoral, particularly if one tells lies during wartime to achieve a strategic goal. He cites Presidents Roosevelt and Lincoln, whose lies during wartime were necessary to achieve their goals. But presidents

"All American presidents have lied – the question is why and when," by Michael Blake, The Conversation, February 16, 2022. https://theconversation.com/all-american-presidents-have-lied-the-question-is-why-and-when-176663. Licensed under CC-BY-ND 4.0 International.

such as Nixon and Clinton, who lied to preserve their own power, are more harshly judged. It is more difficult for presidents to get away with lying in the 21st century, Blake writes, because of social media and dedicated fact-checking. Nowadays, he concludes, it is not enough to lie for political reasons: a president must lie well. Michael Blake is a professor of philosophy, public policy, and governance at the University of Washington.

As you read, consider the following questions:

1. What was philosopher Immanuel Kant's view on lying?
2. How have modern philosophers amended Kant's strict view of lying?
3. How did falsehoods by Roosevelt and Lincoln help achieve their wartime goals?

Those who dislike a president tend to emphasize the frequency or skill with which he lies.

During the Trump administration, for instance, *The Washington Post* kept a running database of the president's lies and deceptions—with the final tally running to over 30,000 falsehoods. President Joe Biden's critics have insisted that he, too, is a liar—and that the media is complicit in ignoring his supposed frequent deception of the American people.

The frequency of these criticisms would seem to indicate that most people do not want a president who lies. And yet a recent study of presidential deception found that all American presidents—from Washington to Trump—have told lies, and knowingly so, in their public statements. The most effective of presidents have sometimes been effective precisely because they were skilled at manipulation and deception.

As a political philosopher with a focus on how people try to reason together through political disagreement, I argue that what matters most is not whether a president lies, but when and why he does so.

Presidents who lie to save their own public image or career are unlikely to be forgiven. However, those who appear to lie in the service of the public are often celebrated.

The Morality of Deception

Why, though, are lies thought so wrongful in the first instance?

Philosopher Immanuel Kant, in the 18th century, provided one powerful account of the wrongness of lying. For Kant, lying was wrong in much the same way that threats and coercion are wrong. All of these override the autonomous will of another person, and treat that person as a mere tool. When a gunman uses threats to coerce a person to do a particular act, he disrespects that person's rational agency. Lies are similarly disrespectful to rational agency: One's decision has been manipulated, so that the act is no longer one's own.

Kant regarded any lie as immoral—even one told to a murderer at the door.

Modern-day philosophers have often endorsed versions of Kant's account while seeking exceptions from its rigidness. One common theme is the necessity of the deception for achieving an important political goal. For example, a political leader who gives honest answers about a forthcoming military operation would likely imperil that operation—and most citizens of the state engaging in that military action would not want that. The key is that people might accept such deception, after the fact, because of what that deception made possible.

During World War II, the British government sought to deceive the Nazi command about its plans for invasion—which entailed lying even to British allies. The moral imperative of defeating Nazi Germany is generally thought to be important enough to justify this sort of deception.

This example also illustrates another theme: Deception might be permitted when it is in the context of an adversarial relationship in which truth-telling should not be expected. Lying to one's own citizens may or may not be justifiable—but there seems to be very little wrong about lying to one's *enemies* during wartime.

Honorable Lies?

These ideas might be used in defense of some presidential lies.

During the 1930s, President Franklin D. Roosevelt was convinced that Hitler's expansionism in Europe was a threat to the liberal democratic project itself, but he faced an electorate without any will to intervene in a European war. Roosevelt chose to insist publicly that he was opposed to any intervention—while doing everything he could to prepare for war and to covertly help the British cause.

As early as 1948, historian Thomas Bailey noted that Roosevelt had made a calculated choice to both prepare for war and insist he was doing no such thing. To be open about his view of Hitler would have likely led to his defeat in the 1940 election.

Before Roosevelt, Abraham Lincoln made similar calculations. Lincoln's lies regarding his negotiations with the Confederacy—described by Meg Mott, a professor of political theory, as being "devious"—may have been instrumental in preserving the United States as a single country.

Lincoln was willing to open peace negotiations with the Confederacy, knowing that much of his own party thought that only unconditional surrender by the South would settle the question of slavery. At one point, Lincoln wrote a note to his own party asserting—falsely—that there were "no peace commissioners" being sent to a conference with the Confederacy.

A member of the Congress later noted that, in the absence of that note, the 13th Amendment—which ended the practice of chattel slavery—would not have been passed.

Good Lies and Bad Lies

The problem, of course, is that a great many presidential lies cannot be so easily linked to important purposes.

President Bill Clinton's lies about his sexual activities were either simply self-serving or told to preserve his presidency.

Similarly, President Richard Nixon's insistence that he knew nothing about the Watergate break-in was most likely a lie. John Dean, Nixon's legal counsel, confirmed years later that the president knew about, and approved of, the plan to rob the Democratic National Committee headquarters. This scandal eventually ended Nixon's presidency.

In both cases, these presidents faced a significant threat to their presidencies—and chose deception to save not the nation, but their own power.

President Biden, President Trump and Truth

It is likely that President Trump lied more than most presidents. What is striking about his lies, however, is that they have tended to be told to defend his own self-image or political viability rather than in service of some central political good.

Indeed, some of President Trump's more implausible lies seemed best understood as tests of loyalty; those in his circle who repeated his most obvious lies demonstrated their loyalty to President Trump in doing so. Most recently, he has attacked as disloyal those members of the Republican Party who have not repeated his false claims about electoral fraud.

Recent studies indicate that President Biden, thus far, has not shown himself equal to President Trump in his deceptiveness. He has, however, made deceptive and misleading claims on a number of topics, ranging from the costs of particular policies to his own history and early life. These lies seem somewhat unlike those told by Lincoln and by Roosevelt; they seem generally told in the interests of making a rhetorical point more powerful rather than as necessary means to an otherwise unobtainable political goal. They seem, in that respect, less morally justifiable than these earlier falsehoods.

A justification for these lies might be found with reference to practices which—like warfare or politics—necessarily involve conflict and gamesmanship. No one would expect honesty from the enemy side during warfare, and perhaps one should not from opponents in politics either. Some political philosophers have thought that, when politics becomes an adversarial game, politicians might be forgiven when they seek to deceive the other party. President Biden might rely upon this idea, and could note that the Republican Party is less open to bipartisan negotiation than at any time in its history.

Even this last justification, however, may not be enough. Lying to one's political opponents might be permitted in an adversarial context. The lies told by presidents are often addressed to constituents, and such deception seems harder to justify.

And finally, even the most important of lies must be believed for it to be justifiable; a lie that is immediately recognized as such is unlikely to achieve the goal justifying that lie. This is an increasingly difficult burden. Modern presidents find it more challenging to lie without having their lies recognized as untrue than presidents serving before the advent of social media and dedicated fact-checking.

If presidents must sometimes lie to defend important political values, then, it seems as though the good president must be both able to lie and able to lie well.

Viewpoint 4

"Presidential whoppers told on the campaign trail are often boasts or trash talk that fool no one and probably aren't intended to. In any case, campaign lies are personal; they're coming from the president, not from the presidency, and thus not from the government."

Government Lying Is Commonplace—and Dangerous

David Luban

David Luban discusses the various types of lies promulgated by governments, and how these lies differ from personal lies. Government lies—which, he states, are really only lies told by people or groups of people—are lies told to achieve an end goal. Luban differentiates presidential personal lies, perhaps told on the campaign trail, and government policy lies, which have the force of an entire system. Such lies, like personal lies, are commonplace, and Luban cites several examples involving torture, warfare, and other extreme situations. Sometimes these lies have legitimate ends, and Luban draws another distinction between policy lies and lies that cover up government wrongdoing. The latter, he says, are always immoral. But even policy lies can be dangerous and erode public trust. Luban's ultimate answer, however impractical, is to stick to the truth. David

"Thoughts on Government Lies," by David Luban, Knight First Amendment Institute at Columbia University, January 25, 2022. Reprinted by permission. https://knightcolumbia.org/blog/thoughts-on-government-lies

Luban is a professor of law and philosophy at Georgetown Law School. His research interests center on moral and legal responsibility in organizational settings, including law firms, government, and the military.

As you read, consider the following questions:

1. How is Hannah Arendt's quote about presidential lying relevant to this viewpoint?
2. What examples of policy lies does Luban cite?
3. How does Luban differentiate between falsehoods and lies?

Governments lie; this comes as a surprise to nobody. But governments can't lie, nor can they tell the truth. *Governments* don't speak at all. *People* speak. And depending on their role in government, and their purpose, and their audience, the terrain of the lies they tell is vast. It ranges from a manager in a state agency writing malicious lies about a former employee in a job reference, to a diplomat dissembling to another government, to the years of lies about "progress" in the Vietnam War coming from the upper reaches of the defense establishment and documented in the Pentagon Papers.

To map the terrain, let's start at its peak, with the president of the United States. The Poynter Institute's PolitiFact website fact-checks politicians and rates their statements on a six-point scale ranging from "true" to "pants on fire." (Along with "pants on fire," the other flavors of falsehood are "mostly false" and "false." For short, call these three categories the *red zone.*)

According to PolitiFact, Barack Obama was in the red zone in nearly a quarter of his 600 fact-checked statements, making him the least dishonest of our past four presidents. For Donald Trump, it was almost three-fourths of his 944 fact-checked statements, with 17 percent in the "pants on fire" category. Joe Biden veers into the red zone 40 percent of the time.

A falsehood isn't necessarily a lie; that depends on whether the speaker knows it is false. Maybe presidents don't know that the statistics they're spouting were cooked and their anecdotes concocted. In her famous essay on lying in politics, Hannah Arendt pointed out that presidents are wholly reliant on their advisers for factual information, which makes the president "an ideal victim of complete manipulation."

Perhaps so, but standing by a falsehood after it's been publicly and persuasively debunked converts a mere mistake into a lie by omission. You said it, you own it. The president commands the bully pulpit, which makes the "You said it, you own it" principle apply with maximum force. By these lights, the fact that even our least mendacious president lied a quarter of the time sets a disturbing benchmark.

Distinctions matter here. Presidential whoppers told on the campaign trail are often boasts or trash talk that fool no one and probably aren't intended to. In any case, campaign lies are personal; they're coming from the president, not from the *presidency,* and thus not from the government.

Presidential *policy* lies are a different matter. Here's an example of a policy lie. In September 2006, President George W. Bush strode into the East Room and publicly confirmed that the CIA had held terrorism suspects in black sites and interrogated them with what he delicately called an "alternative set of procedures"—which we now know meant torturing them. ("I cannot describe the methods used—I think you understand why.")

Bush's speech was a sales pitch for the program, and his chief selling point was the supposedly lifesaving information the CIA obtained. He offered specific examples to make the sales pitch stronger. The trouble is, they weren't true. His information came from the CIA—but the president stood by it. He said it and he owned it.

What makes it a policy lie is that torture was his government's policy, and nearly every high official had signed off on it: the vice president, the secretaries of defense and state, the national security advisor, the CIA director, the attorney general, and all their lawyers. The fictitious Tonkin Gulf Incident, used to get Congress to approve the Vietnam War without declaring war, was a policy lie. So were the massive falsehoods detailed in the Pentagon Papers, to perpetuate a war that had lost all purpose except to maintain the mirage of "credibility" that fooled no one. And so were the "fixed" intelligence findings used to justify the Iraq War. It may be that some U.S. officials, like Colin Powell and perhaps Bush himself, actually believed that Saddam Hussein had weapons of mass destruction. After all, the government spent two years hunting for them—in vain.

This proves only that Arendt was right when she observed the connection between deception and self-deception. Indeed, government mendacity would hardly have surprised Arendt, who said that "the deliberate falsehood and the outright lie used as legitimate means to achieve political ends, have been with us since the beginning of recorded history." Most people, I think, would agree with her historical claim, but calling policy lies a *legitimate* means should give us pause. What's so legitimate about lying to the public in a democracy, where government is supposed to be accountable to its people? Democratic accountability requires their active and informed opinion, and government lying defeats it.

Again, some distinctions are essential. Obviously, even democratic governments need secrecy and confidentiality for some of their business, and keeping secrets may require lies. In this category, clandestine operations, covert actions, and counterintelligence are the obvious examples. They fall into a class of their own because concealment is built into the nature of the work. Every reader of John le Carré knows that intelligence work takes place in a moral twilight zone, and some covert actions are thoroughly immoral. But intelligence gathering is a fundamental responsibility of government, and its necessary lies can indeed be legitimate. (A recent book by the philosopher Cécile Fabre makes that case well.)

At the opposite end of the spectrum are lies told to cover up government misconduct, malfeasance, or outright criminality. These, I think, are never legitimate. Unfortunately, the temptation to masquerade cover-ups as legitimate state secrets is overwhelming, and our own government has abused the state secrets privilege massively. (My colleague Laura Donohue has documented just how massively.) Even the Supreme Court's leading case establishing the state secrets privilege turned out years later to be based on a cover-up.

I think that Arendt had a third category in mind, and this is the one I find most troubling. All political action rests on persuasion, and in a large, vibrant, and pluralistic country every significant policy will face bitter opposition. Truth, Arendt argued, always appears in public as just another opinion. It won't persuade everyone, and the frictional force of public opinion can lead to paralysis. That's when the temptation toward policy lies is the strongest, and it's at least possible that sometimes the political ends justify lies as the means.

Sometimes. Perhaps. But policy lying is addictive, and a public sphere filled with government lies leads (as Arendt also predicted) to a cynical public that devalues truth and believes nothing—the ultimate political danger to democracy. So, if we have to choose between a hard rule of political morality that forbids government policy lying and a soft permission that threatens to debase truth itself, the choice is easy: Stick to the truth.

Viewpoint 5

> *"Lies are part of the DNA of modern society, though we often now refer to them with the more dignified terminology of marketing, advertising, propaganda or spin."*

How Politicians Delegitimize the Truth

Vittorio Bufacchi

Vittorio Bufacchi writes about how firmly lies are entrenched in our culture. He discusses our "post truth" world, in which the very nature of truth itself is called into question. Bufacchi compares lies told by Presidents Clinton and Trump. The former's lies were disturbing and inexcusable, but the latter's were dangerous, he claims. Trump is not merely lying, Bufacchi asserts; instead, he is undermining "the theoretical infrastructure that makes it possible to have a conversation about the truth." We can tolerate politicians lying, Bufacchi concludes, but we cannot allow them to alter the very nature of the meaning of truth. Vittorio Bufacchi is senior lecturer in the department of philosophy at University College Cork in Ireland. His book Everything Must Change: Philosophical Lessons from Lockdown *was published by Manchester University Press in 2021.*

"What's the difference between lies and post-truth in politics? A philosopher explains," by Vittorio Bufacchi, The Conversation, January 24, 2020. https://theconversation.com/whats-the-difference-between-lies-and-post-truth-in-politics-a-philosopher-explains-130442. Licensed under CC-BY-ND 4.0 International.

As you read, consider the following questions:

1. Why does Bufacchi cite the "liar's paradox" to begin this viewpoint?
2. How does a lie differ from "post truth," according to the viewpoint?
3. According to Bufacchi, why is Trump's undermining of the meaning of truth so dangerous?

If I wrote "The first sentence in this article is a lie," is this sentence true, or is it a lie? And, if a liar declares "I am lying," is the liar telling the truth? In philosophy and logic this is known as the Liar's Paradox: the liar is a liar, and if the liar is indeed lying, then the liar is telling the truth, which means the liar just lied.

Lies are part of the DNA of modern society, though we often now refer to them with the more dignified terminology of marketing, advertising, propaganda or spin. From unscrupulous sellers of used cars to prime ministers making unsubstantiated declarations about weapons of mass destruction, it seems that many people now make a living from lies.

In the public imagination politicians are professional liars par excellence, or as the writer George Orwell once put it: "Political language … is designed to make lies sound truthful and murder respectable."

In her essay "Truth and Politics," published in *The New Yorker* in 1967, the philosopher Hannah Arendt was already lamenting the fact that politics and truth don't mix. But even Arendt was aware that not all lies are the same. There are lies that are minimal forms of deception, a micro-tear in the fabric of reality, while some lies are so big that they require a complete rearrangement of the whole factual texture, a shift to another reality. In today's terminology, Arendt was alerting us to the difference between a lie, and the 2016 Oxford Dictionaries Word of the Year—"post-truth."

One way to understand the difference between lies and post-truth, which I've written about in a new paper, is that a liar denies specific facts that have precise coordinates in space and time, whereas post-truth questions the very nature of truth. A liar knows the truth, and, by trying to persuade us of an alternative narrative, a liar is paradoxically honouring the truth, whereas post-truth allows no last refuge for the truth.

Clinton Versus Trump

This distinction between a lie and post-truth becomes more clear by comparing two recent American presidents, Bill Clinton and Donald Trump. At a White House press conference on January 26 1998, Clinton famously said:

> *I want to say one thing to the American people. I want you to listen to me. I'm going to say this again: I did not have sexual relations with that woman, Miss Lewinsky. I never told anybody to lie, not a single time; never.*

Clinton's statement, given the subsequent revelations and a semen-stained blue dress, is disconcerting. It's possible that Clinton did not consider his intimate interactions with Lewinsky as a "sexual relation," but that is unlikely—it would require a phenomenal effort of self-deception, or ingenuity, to defend that position with honesty and integrity. Clinton was impeached for perjury and obstruction of justice, because he lied under oath, but he was ultimately acquitted in a Senate trial.

Subverting Truth Itself

Clinton lied, and that was inexcusable. But Trump's relationship with truth is even more disturbing, and dangerous. Trump's incessant accusations of fake news against the main media outlets, including the *Washington Post*, *The New York Times*, and CNN, reflects a longstanding disdain for the truth. Unlike Clinton, Trump is not simply denying certain facts, instead he is determined to undermine the theoretical infrastructure that makes it possible to have a conversation about the truth.

Trump's response and demeanour to the impeachment allegations made against him is a typical example of post-truth. By spurning the impeachment proceedings as a "charade" and a "witch-hunt," his strategy is to create an environment where objective facts are less influential in shaping public opinion, where theoretical frameworks necessary to make sense of certain events are scorned, and where scientific truth is delegitimised.

This is the major difference between a lie and post-truth. While a lie subverts a specific truth, post-truth tries to subvert truth itself. Trump's abhorrence of truth is reflected in the remarkable claim by one of his lawyers, Rudy Giuliani, that "truth is relative." Giuliani was talking on NBC News about the request by special counsel Robert Mueller for an interview with Trump regarding the Russia investigation. Giuliani raised concerns that Trump could perjure himself because "truth isn't truth."

Post-truth is a murky concept, but it should not be confused with a lie. Post-truth is much more devious and dangerous to the democratic fabric of our society. The prefix "post" in post-truth refers to the claim that a specified idea has become redundant and therefore can safely be discarded. Post-truth is the belief that truth is no longer essential, that truth has become obsolete.

We can cope with politicians lying, but we cannot afford the risk of allowing politicians to deligitimise truth.

Periodical and Internet Sources Bibliography

The following articles have been selected to supplement the diverse views presented in this chapter.

Gwenda Blair, "Opinion: Donald Trump Betrayed the Country. And It Worked." *Politico*, May 12, 2023. https://www.politico.com/news/magazine/2023/05/12/trump-betrayal-00094766.

Ullrich Ecker and Toby Prike, "We know politicians lie—but do we care?" The Conversation, February 13, 2022. https://theconversation.com/we-know-politicians-lie-but-do-we-care-176578.

Alison Escalante, "Dishonest Candidates Win Elections, According to New Research," *Forbes*, October 13, 2020. https://www.forbes.com/sites/alisonescalante/2020/10/13/dishonest-candidates-win-elections-according-to-new-research/?sh=33e73cae24b9.

Federico Finchelstein, "A Brief History of Fascist Lies," *BookForum*, April 21, 2020. https://www.bookforum.com/politics/how-political-lying-leads-to-violence-23980.

Ben Glaze. "Exclusive: Lying by politicians should be made a specific criminal offence, say voters," *Mirror,* May 5, 2021. https://www.mirror.co.uk/news/politics/lying-politicians-should-made-specific-24045115.

Gaby Hinsliff, "The Lies of the Land: A Brief History of Political Dishonesty by Adam Macqueen – Review," the *Guardian*, September 3, 2017. https://www.theguardian.com/books/2017/sep/03/lies-of-land-brief-history-political-dishonesty-adam-macqueen-review.

Nigel Hogan, "Under What Circumstances Is It Legitimate for Politicians to Lie?," E-International Relations, August 22, 2012. https://www.e-ir.info/2012/08/22/under-what-circumstances-is-it-legitimate-for-politicians-to-lie/.

John Humphrys, "Honesty in politics: an over-rated virtue?," YouGov UK, September 10, 2021. https://yougov.co.uk/topics/politics/articles-reports/2021/09/10/honesty-politics-over-rated-virtue.

Bill Lueders, "Lies, Lies, and More Lies: A Presidential History," the *Progressive Magazine*, August 10, 2020. https://progressive.org/latest/lies-more-lies-presidential-history-lueders-200810/.

Aja Romano, "Conspiracy theories, explained," *Vox*, November 18, 2020. https://www.vox.com/21558524/conspiracy-theories-2020-qanon-covid-conspiracies-why.

Sophia Rosenfeld, "Is Lying Actually a Good Thing in Politics?," Knight First Amendment Institute at Columbia University, September 21, 2021. https://knightcolumbia.org/blog/lies-and-the-law-is-lying-actually-a-good-thing-in-politics.

David Schultz, "Is it Ever Ethical for Public Officials to Lie in the Name of the Public Good?," *International Policy Digest*, April 8, 2020. https://intpolicydigest.org/is-it-ever-ethical-for-public-officials-to-lie-in-the-name-of-the-public-good/.

Opposing Viewpoints® Series

Chapter 4

Is Political Lobbying an Ethical System?

Chapter Preface

For the average American citizen, dependence on government institutions is a necessity. Laws are written every day that affect our health, our wealth, and our general wellbeing. We send representatives to local, state, and national government knowing that they will write legislation that will affect our lives—after all, this is their job. They are called legislators for a reason.

Short of phoning our elected representatives, or writing an email, or voicing our opinion on social media, there is little one can do besides voting and hoping to affect such legislation—unless, of course, we are wealthy and powerful enough to hire lobbyists who will do the job for us. But the average person can no more affect legislation than they can walk on the moon. Lobbyists can shape legislation, and do so every day of the year. Moreover, if recent investigative journalism reports are to be believed, lobbyists actually write legislation.

According to the organization the Center for Public Integrity, "Each year, state lawmakers across the U.S. introduce thousands of bills dreamed up and written by corporations, industry groups and think tanks." The practice is apparently common knowledge in Congress, though not among ordinary citizens. *USA TODAY*, the *Arizona Republic,* and the Center for Public Integrity conducted a two-year study of corporate lawmaking, and the results were astounding. Such proposed legislation, written not by legislators but by their corporate constituents, are called "model" bills. "Disguised as the work of lawmakers, these so-called 'model' bills get copied in one state Capitol after another, quietly advancing the agenda of the people who write them." The study found that over 10,000 bills were copied word-for-word from model legislation and introduced nationwide during a recent eight-year-period. More than 2,100 of those bills were signed into law.

Perhaps these lobbyists and lawmakers have the best of intentions. Perhaps they feel as former French President Charles

De Gaulle did when he said, "I have come to the conclusion that politics is too serious a matter to be left to the politicians." But it is more likely that they have their own best interests in mind. As former U.S. Congressman Marty Meehan has said, "Real lobbying reform must end the practice of corporate lobbyists writing our laws."

Most lobbyists are not advocating—or writing—legislation to benefit the public good. They are pushing for laws that will benefit their corporations, and, more often than not, their corporations' bottom line. As is so often the case, lobbying is about money. Millions of dollars are spent on lobbying Congress each year so that corporations can rake in billions. Money begets money in our political system. And it's all legal. If a company doesn't want to adhere to a law because following it will cost them money, they send lobbyists who will ask legislators to cut them a break. According to Josh Fox, American film director, playwright, and environmental activist, best known for his 2010 documentary *Gasland*, "The gas industry spent $250 million getting an exemption from our Safe Water Act. Every one of those dollars is toxic; a contaminant in our political system. [Such lobbying] disrupts the normal flow of justice, science, fact and reporting."

The more powerful the organization, the more they can affect legislation. Financial institutions are a case in point. According to Senator Bernie Sanders, "Wall Street is clearly the most powerful lobbying force on Capitol Hill. From 1998 through 2008, the financial sector spent over $5 billion in lobbying and campaign contributions to deregulate Wall Street." One can draw a straight line between this deregulation and the financial crisis of 2008 that caused so much hardship for the average American.

The practice of lobbying is not going away. The best the ordinary American citizen can hope for is that legislators will find the courage to scrutinize and police the system more effectively. But where large sums of money are concerned, such oversight may never overcome corporate greed or rein in politicians driven by money and power.

Viewpoint 1

> *"Wealthy companies can move money around the globe instantly and anonymously, in official currencies or in cryptocurrencies, issued by no state. They can use this invisible money to purchase the services of lobbyists, or to donate to political campaigns, in ways that are almost impossible to trace."*

Big Data Gives the Wealthy and Powerful More Ability to Lobby Politicians

Phil Parvin

Phil Parvin writes about how the advent of advanced data systems has allowed big corporations to supercharge their lobbying efforts. New technologies have allowed the wealthy to increase their access to political power in ways that couldn't have been imagined previously. They can use cryptocurrencies and other untraceable money in order to buy the services of lobbyists or to donate to political campaigns. For example, a service such as FiscalNote uses artificial intelligence to gather data on politicians, regulations, and public policy developments. With this data they can provide wealthy clients with up-to-the-minute information that they can use to target politicians and generate grassroots support. Their clients, Parvin writes, are some of the richest companies on

"21st-century lobbying: how big data lets big businesses get the upper hand," by Phil Parvin, The Conversation, October 18, 2019. https://theconversation.com/21st-century-lobbying-how-big-data-lets-big-businesses-get-the-upper-hand-121918. Licensed under CC-BY-ND 4.0 International.

the planet. Big data and new technology, Parvin states, have allowed such companies to extend their dominance and grow even richer. Phil Parvin is a reader in politics and Director of Research for Politics and International Studies and Chair of the Ethics in Public Life Research Group at Loughborough University.

As you read, consider the following questions:

1. How much did Google's expenditure on lobbying increase between 2002 and 2017?
2. How, according to Parvin, does new technology give major corporations an edge in shaping our politics?
3. Why can't government regulators keep up with the new technologies?

In July Facebook was fined US$5.1bn by the US Federal Trade Commission (FTC) for not being honest about how it was handling user data. The personal data of 87 million of its users had been harvested by Cambridge Analytica, a firm which stands accused of building political profiles of individual people in order to influence elections. It is believed that the information was used to influence voters in the U.S. presidential election and the EU referendum of 2016.

The fine is the biggest ever handed down by the FTC. It certainly sounds like a lot, but it isn't. Facebook's Q2 earnings, reported the same week, were a better-than-expected $16.9bn. The fine is the amount of money Facebook makes in 27 days. Facebook investors are relieved. Its share price has risen.

The same week, Brexit Party leader Nigel Farage launched World4Brexit, a US-based fundraising operation aimed at enabling "friends of the UK from around the world" to donate to the ongoing campaign to ensure that the UK leaves the EU. World4Brexit is based in Michigan and is a registered non-profit organisation, which means that it can accept individual donations of up to $5,000 without having to name donors.

The Labour Party has called for an investigation following concerns that the organisation will allow foreign "dark money" to subvert the democratic process. Similar concerns have been raised about the Brexit Party possibly receiving donations through Paypal in ways that don't comply with UK electoral law.

Even if the Labour Party gets its investigation, nothing much will happen. These two events dramatise a tension between money and politics that is unique to the 21st century.

The Benefits of Lobbying

Lobbying is the process of trying to influence key policymakers. Lobbyists will attempt to educate public officials to take a stand that best aligns with the interest of who they are representing. While it is true that big corporations spend billions of dollars on lobbying, any kind of business, large or small, can hire and benefit from a lobbyists' extensive knowledge in a variety of subject areas.

Anyone from big corporations to individuals and non-profits to unions can utilize lobbying services. More and more groups are hiring lobbyists to represent them and have their voices be heard. But one question remains, is lobbying good or bad for democracy? Here are a couple of reasons why lobbying is an essential part of a working government and democracy.

Lobbying Is Protected Under the First Amendment

While there is no place in the Constitution that specifically states or mentions the word "lobbying," it is protected under the 1st Amendment, stating that "Congress shall make no law abridging the freedom to petition the government for a redress of grievances." This means

Bigger Business, Deeper Pockets

Wealthy individuals and organisations have a disproportionate influence over elected representatives. This has long been the case, and certainly predates the rise of companies such as Facebook, Google and Cambridge Analytica. But the amount of money these companies have to spend is unprecedented. Apple was the first company to be valued at more than $1 trillion. Alphabet (Google's parent company) is worth around $900bn; Facebook $560bn. The world's ten richest corporations now own more wealth than the poorest 180 states combined.

As the wealth of these corporations has grown, so the amount they've spent on lobbying has grown too. In 2002, for example, Google spent less than $50,000 on lobbying Washington. In 2017, it spent $18m—more than any other company in the

that the people have the right to petition the government and have their voices heard on topics that affect them.

Lobbying Gives a Voice to The Unrepresented

Most people do not have the time, resources, or skills to present themselves in front of policymakers and advocate for their interests. Lobbyists give people the opportunity to be represented in front of these public officials and get a seat at the discussion table. Lobbyists give these individuals, companies, non-profits, and worker unions a voice. Providing them with a chance to give their input, and raise their concerns regarding policies that affect them.

Lobbyists Provide Educational Insights

With over 10,000 bills presented to Congress, it is hard to imagine that policymakers are experts in every subject. Since lobbyists often specialize in specific subject areas, they can represent and articulate the interests of their clients as experts in the matter. Therefore, lobbyists can also educate and bring to light issues that public officials might be unfamiliar with, providing benefits to both parties.

"Is Lobbying Good or Bad for Democracy?," Dorn Policy Group, November 5, 2020.

world. In 2018, it spent $21m. Google also spent more money than any other corporation in the U.S. on political donations in the 2016 presidential election

The use of lobbyists by corporations is widespread. Non-corporate organisations haven't been able to keep up. For every $1 spent on lobbying by labour unions and public interest groups combined in 2015, $34 was spent by large corporations and the associations which represent them.

The New Technology of Lobbying

There is nothing especially new in corporations translating their wealth into political power or in the fact that power is concentrated among wealthy organisations and individuals.

What is new is that technologies have emerged which concentrate power in the hands of the wealthy and increase inequality of access—on a scale unimaginable only a few years ago. Wealthy companies can move money around the globe instantly and anonymously, in official currencies or in cryptocurrencies, issued by no state. They can use this invisible money to purchase the services of lobbyists, or to donate to political campaigns, in ways that are almost impossible to trace. And they can access information that can be used to bolster their lobbying efforts in ways not open to poorer individuals and organisations.

Human civilisation now has greater access to information than at any point in its history. In an ideal world, this fact should be liberating and empowering. It should enrich democracy, inform citizens and make for a more reflective and egalitarian politics. But we don't live in an ideal world.

We live in a world in which information—and the expertise necessary to analyse it—comes at a price that only wealthy organisations can pay. From the outside, lobbying may look the same as it always has, but it isn't – it's driven increasingly by an information divide. A divide between those who can afford it and those who can't.

If you want to glimpse this, take a look at the new niche industry which has emerged to help companies leverage complex data in the service of supplying political intelligence and altering the political agenda.

FiscalNote is an example. Based in the U.S., it uses "artificial intelligence, machine learning, and natural language processing" to scrape the internet for data on politicians, regulations and public policy developments in order to provide paying clients with up-to-the-minute data they can use to target politicians and mobilise grassroots support.

Its clients are some of the wealthiest companies on Earth, including Nestlé, the world's largest food company ($247bn), Nouryon, the Dutch chemical company ($5bn), and the U.S. Corn Growers Association, which represents the interests of the U.S. field corn and ethanol industry ($50bn). FiscalNote charges between $US10,000 and "several hundred thousand dollars" a year to enable organisations that can afford it to achieve lobbying successes far beyond what smaller, less resourced organisations can achieve.

We all know now that new technologies have made it easier than ever to influence elections, and to move money around the world in ways which are harder to trace. What's less visible is the extent to which they have made it easier for the wealthy to lobby more effectively for their interests.

Big data hasn't levelled the playing field. It has simply allowed wealthy organisations and individuals to further entrench their dominance. And regulators can't keep up. New technologies make it almost impossible to trace the global flow of money World4Brexit may receive to fund its political campaigning. The FTC's stern rebuke of Facebook was nothing of the kind. Institutions are scrambling, and failing, to keep pace with the technological changes shaping our politics.

Viewpoint 2

> *"Lobbying on climate change by companies often conjures up the image of covert, anti-regulatory activities that subvert the public interest."*

Lobbyists Can Play a Crucial Role in Helping to Meet Climate Change Goals

Rory Sullivan, Robert Black, Richard Perkins, and Clare Richards

In this viewpoint, the authors discuss the current state of climate change lobbying and the manner in which various companies lobby governments. The authors identify two types of lobbying: direct lobbying, which involves direct contact between the lobbying party and public policy decision-makers; and indirect lobbying, where the lobbying party seeks to influence public policy by shaping and gaining support from the public and other stakeholders. The authors point out how climate lobbying can have major negative impacts. Climate lobbying can be self-serving to companies that do not want to change their practices. The authors conclude by offering recommendations about how lobbying can help meet the goals of the Paris Agreement and have a beneficial impact on climate change instead. Rory Sullivan is CEO at Chronos Sustainability and visiting professor in practice at the Grantham Research Institute. Robert Black is the Head of Responsible Investment at Chronos Sustainability.

"What role should institutional investors be taking in the governance of corporate climate change lobbying?," by Rory Sullivan, Robert Black, Richard Perkins, and Clare Richards, London School of Economics, February 25, 2022. Reprinted by permission.

Richard Perkins is an associate professor in the department of geography and environment at the London School of Economics. Clare Richards is Senior Engagement Manager at the Church of England Pensions Board.

As you read, consider the following questions:

1. According to the authors, why is a wider conception of lobbying important to acknowledge?
2. How does their definition of lobbying relate to this wider conception?
3. What specific recommendations do the authors make to ensure that lobbyists help countries reach the goals set in the Paris Agreement?

Despite a range of initiatives by governments, companies and civil actors, it is widely recognised that global collective action on climate change is currently inconsistent with full implementation of the Paris Agreement.

It is also recognised that a substantial ratcheting up of policy ambition and commitments is needed, and that this would entail major changes in many economic sectors, creating opportunities in some and significant downside risks in others (e.g. in the oil and gas sector).

In the face of such significant impacts, some companies have lobbied governments for regulations and policies that help the private sector to contribute to domestic and international climate change goals. However, some companies, particularly in high-carbon sectors, have chosen to lobby to maintain the current regulatory status quo, to delay change and to call for limited action that would be insufficient to meet the goals of the Paris Agreement. It is against this backdrop that companies' lobbying activities should be assessed.

The lobbying activities of companies have taken on an added significance since the Paris Agreement emerged from the United Nations climate change summit in December 2015. Since the Agreement came into force on 4 November 2016, 192 countries have deposited with the United Nations their instruments of ratification, acceptance, approval or accession. These countries are now bound by the Agreement and many are starting to embed its goals into domestic policies and legislation.

This policy brief describes the nature and characteristics of climate lobbying by companies and its influence on climate change policy. From this analysis, it offers recommendations to private and public actors on how to govern climate lobbying by companies so that this lobbying does not undermine implementation of the Paris Agreement.

Adopting a Broad Definition of Climate Lobbying

The academic and practitioner literature identifies two general categories of lobbying:

- Direct lobbying, involving direct contact between the lobbying party and public policy decision-makers; and
- Indirect lobbying, where the lobbying party seeks to influence public policy by shaping and mobilising support from the public and other stakeholders.

There is agreement that direct contact with policymakers constitutes lobbying, but not all definitions, including those enshrined in public regulation, include indirect influence.

We argue that a broad definition should be adopted, given that companies, and their agents and affiliates, lobby directly and indirectly, with the aims of shaping understanding and perceptions of climate change science, policy and/or the opportunities and risks for companies. As policy decision-making on climate change is shaped by both public opinion and interest group representation, this wider conception of lobbying is necessary to capture important forms of influence by companies.

We therefore consider lobbying on climate change by companies as:

Activities carried out by companies or their agents to directly or indirectly influence climate-related policy decision-making by political or bureaucratic actors

This definition covers the entire policy life cycle. It encompasses all policies that—directly or indirectly, explicitly or implicitly—deal with climate change mitigation, adaptation, loss and damage or disaster risk management. It includes domestic lobbying as well as the lobbying of international organisations such as the secretariat of the United Nations Framework Convention on Climate Change.

Understanding Lobbying in Practice

Distinguishing Between Positive and Negative Lobbying

Lobbying on climate change by companies often conjures up the image of covert, anti-regulatory activities that subvert the public interest. Indeed, academic research suggests that "anti-regulatory" lobbying by companies, their agents and their associations, alliances and coalitions can succeed in impeding the adoption, stringency and implementation of public climate policy (e.g. see Stokes, 2020). It can benefit those with the resources to lobby effectively, while those without the same resources or level of political influence may find themselves penalised.

Climate lobbying can have major negative economic impacts. One example is the success of the lobbying against the Waxman-Markey Bill (formally the American Clean Energy and Security Act), which failed to make it through the U.S. Senate in 2010. The global social cost of the failure of this bill, which proposed a 17% cut in U.S. emissions by 2020, an 80% cut by 2050 and the introduction of a national cap-and-trade emissions trading scheme (among other elements), was estimated at US$467bn (in 2018 US dollars) (Meng and Rode, 2019). Lobbying by companies has been estimated to have increased the likelihood of the bill not passing by 13%. Therefore—in this case alone—lobbying by companies could have cost society as a whole US$60bn (ibid.).

Even in the relatively narrowly defined frame of a company's own self-interest, opposing climate policy may have negative results. For example, anti-regulatory lobbying may undermine the company's reputation for sustainability or corporate responsibility, and may result in insufficient focus on how it might respond to the technology, market and policy/legal risks associated with climate change or on how it will deal with the physical impacts.

It is important to acknowledge that some lobbying by companies may support effective action on climate change. A well-documented example is pro-regulatory lobbying by some businesses which contributed to the adoption of the EU's emissions trading system (ETS) (Meckling, 2011).

Principles for Responsible Lobbying

The issues around lobbying include how it is undertaken, the ends it serves and, critically, the relationship between the means and the ends. Several practitioner frameworks for responsible lobbying have been developed, comprising various "best practice" principles.1 Box 2 presents the principles[1] that have been commonly identified.

Regarding the "ends," an important question is whether lobbying is aligned with the goals of the Paris Agreement. This needs to look beyond the "obvious" climate-related lobbying (e.g. for or against fossil fuel subsidies) to encompass the full range of outcomes and consequences of lobbying.

For example, academic research suggests that some forms of apparently pro-regulatory lobbying may in fact be largely self-serving and strategic: companies may, for instance, call to substitute more demanding climate policy action with less stringent alternatives in order to reduce perceived compliance costs (Ferns and Amaeshi, 2019; Grumbach, 2017).

Numerous and Varying Practices and Tactics

Companies may seek to influence policy in a variety of ways. Most of the academic studies have focused on Europe, North America or Australasia. Less is known about how climate lobbying by companies takes place outside these regions (a notable exception is Trencher et al., 2020). These gaps suggest that we need to be sensitive to geographical variations in tactics and practices, and to be careful not to apply an overly rigid or narrow taxonomy of lobbying activities.

Influence of Trade Associations, and Industry Alliances and Coalitions

Trade associations, and industry alliances and coalitions, are widely identified as key actors involved in climate lobbying by companies (see, for example, InfluenceMap 2017, 2021). These organisations can increase the weight policymakers give to companies' views—particularly if they can demonstrate sectoral unity. Some trade associations have been criticised for allowing individual high-carbon companies to publicly distance themselves from controversial lobbying positions that they support, for enabling larger high-carbon companies to exert undue influence, and for a lack of transparency over how policy positions are reached (ibid.).

Trade associations may also lobby in support of climate-related policy (e.g. see Gullberg, 2013). It is also interesting that a number of major energy companies have—often in response to investor pressure—recently published reviews of the climate lobbying activities of their trade associations, and that these reviews have led to them withdrawing from or suspending their membership of some of these groups (see, for example, Anglo American, 2021; Shell, 2021).

Lobbying During Implementation of Climate Legislation

Companies lobby both prior to and after the formal adoption of climate laws. Such lobbying may be especially significant in the case of overarching climate laws and other legal instruments where many of the policy details are worked out later on. A well-documented example of such "post-decisional" lobbying arose in the aforementioned case of the EU ETS, where anti-regulatory lobbying efforts were successful in weakening and reducing its effectiveness (Martin et al., 2010).

Consistency in Responsible Lobbying

Consistency emerges as a critical principle in the academic literature and practitioner guidance. Its importance stems from the observation that there may be a significant disparity between firms' external communication and marketing around corporate social responsibility (CSR) and their approach to political activity—including in climate-related areas (Favotto and Kollman, 2019). Consistency implies close alignment between a firm's stated climate position, its own lobbying activities and those of third-party affiliates (e.g. trade associations). Inconsistency can come from a lack of overarching governance structures to ensure messaging from differing departments and lobbying activity is aligned.

Implications and Recommendations for Policy

We make five recommendations to private and public actors seeking to govern climate lobbying by companies.

Recommendation 1: Investors Should Create a Clear and Consistent Definition of Climate Lobbying

A clear definition of what climate lobbying encapsulates would enable investors and other stakeholders to better hold lobbyists to account, signify clear actions for lobbying (e.g. joint interventions) and support governance frameworks for responsible lobbying. Any such definition should encompass both direct and indirect lobbying.

Recommendation 2: Companies Should Publish Annual Political Impact Statements

Any company that carries out direct or indirect lobbying in relation to climate change should outline, annually, its lobbying activity, including that of its agents, its trade associations and the alliances and coalitions of which it is a member. Each such company should provide an assessment of how those activities have impacted the adoption and/or implementation of climate change policy and the extent to which these have helped meet the stated aims of the Paris Agreement. Where there is misalignment between lobbying activity and a company's public position on climate change, it should be attendant on the firm to explain the discrepancy. The company should also describe its lobbying governance and oversight processes, and explain how it ensures that its lobbying activities are consistent with the Paris Agreement.

Recommendation 3: Investors Should Develop Lobbying Metrics

There is a need for more transparency around companies' political activity, both direct and indirect lobbying. To this end, metrics are required that allow lobbying activity to be objectively assessed by stakeholders including investors, and the effectiveness of companies' governance frameworks to be evaluated. In the EU, policymakers could consider adding such metrics to the proposals for a Corporate Sustainability Reporting Directive.

Recommendation 4: Companies Should Consider Supporting and Normalising Lobbying in Support of Effective Climate Policies

Conceptions of responsible climate lobbying should move beyond the principle of not lobbying in a way that is contrary to the public interest. Under an expanded view of corporate political responsibility, companies with the requisite capabilities ought to actively consider whether they can and should lobby in support of the adoption and timely implementation of effective climate policies that meet the aims of the Paris Agreement. Companies should also consider lobbying to ensure climate concerns are integrated into non-environmental policies.

Governments should consider mechanisms for ensuring the transparency of lobbying on climate change by companies, and if necessary, incorporate these into practices and regulations. For example, the European Commission has described the aim of its efforts on sustainable corporate governance as being to: "improve the EU regulatory framework on company law and corporate governance. It would enable companies to focus on long-term sustainable value creation rather than short-term benefits. It aims to better align the interests of companies, their shareholders, managers, stakeholders and society" (European Commission, 2021).

Recommendation 5: Companies Should Support Collective Action in Support of the Goals of the Paris Agreement

The Paris Agreement has now been ratified, accepted or approved by almost 200 countries around the world. Companies based in these countries should consider themselves to be bound by the Paris Agreement and committed to its implementation. Meeting the goals of the Paris Agreement requires collective action. As part of their responsibilities, companies should ally themselves with other concerned stakeholders, to create supportive coalitions for effective climate action—acknowledging that there may be practical challenges, such as competition law constraints and the feasibility of collaborating with competitors, which may limit this ambition. Such coalitions should actively support effective domestic climate policy in line with the Paris Agreement.

Conclusions

Lobbying should be understood as important to developing an effective regulatory environment that is consistent with the goals of the Paris Agreement. It is incumbent on those companies that carry out direct and indirect climate lobbying, along with their agents, their trade associations, and their industry alliances and coalitions, to aim to further effective climate policy in line with the goals of the Paris Agreement. Lobbying activities must also become more transparent, enabling scrutiny and evaluation by other relevant stakeholders, thereby enhancing the accountability of companies.

References

Anglo American (2021) *Anglo American Industry Association Audit, April 2021,* Ceres, Boston

Ceres (2020) *Blueprint for Responsible Policy Engagement on Climate Change* European Commission (2021) *Sustainable Corporate Governance*

Fagan-Watson B, Elliott B, Watson T (2015) *Lobbying by Trade Associations on EU Climate Policy,* University of Westminster, London

Favotto A, Kollman K (2019) Mixing Business with Politics: Does Corporate Social Responsibility End Where Lobbying Transparency Begins? *Regulation & Governance* 15(4)

Ferns G, Amaeshi K (2019) Fueling Climate (In)Action: How Organizations Engage in Hegemonization to Avoid Transformational Action on Climate Change. *Organization Studies*, 42(7): 1005-1029

Grumbach J M (2017) Polluting industries as climate protagonists: cap and trade and the problem of business preferences. *Business and Politics*, 17(4): 633-659

Gullberg A T (2013) Pressure or Information? Lobbying for Binding Renewable Energy Targets in the European Union. *Review of Policy Research*, 30(6): 611-628

InfluenceMap (2017) *Trade Associations and their Climate Policy Footprint* InfluenceMap (2021) *Industry Associations and European Climate Ambition*

Institutional Investor Group on Climate Change [IIGCC] (2018) *European Investor Expectations on Corporate Lobbying on Climate Change*

Martin R, Muûls M, Wagner U J (2010) *Policy Brief: Still time to reclaim the European Union Emissions Trading System for the European tax payer.* Centre for Economic Performance, London School of Economics and Political Science

Meckling J (2011) *Carbon Coalitions: Business, Climate Politics, and the Rise of Emissions Trading*, MIT Press, Cambridge, MA

Meng K C, Rode A (2019) The Social Cost of Lobbying over Climate Policy. *Nature Climate Change*, 9(6): 472-476

Principles for Responsible Investment [PRI] (2018) *Investor Expectations on Corporate Climate Lobbying*

Shell (2021) *Industry Associations Climate Review 2021*

Stokes L C (2020) *Short Circuiting Policy: Interest Groups and the Battle over Clean Energy and Climate Policy in the American States,* Oxford University Press, Oxford

Transparency International (2015) *Responsible Lobbying: A Short Guide to Ethical Lobbying and Public Policy Engagement for Professionals, Executives and Activists*

Trencher G, Rinscheid A, Duygan M, Truong N, Asuka J (2020) Revisiting Carbon Lock-in in Energy Systems: Explaining the Perpetuation of Coal Power in Japan. *Energy Research & Social Science*, 69, 101770

UN Global Compact [UNGC], World Resources Institute, CDP, WWF, Ceres, The Climate Group (2013) *Caring for Climate: Guide for Responsible Corporate Engagement in Climate Policy*

Viewpoint 3

> *"We know less about state and local government lobbying in Washington than we do about other types."*

Not Enough Is Known About How Local and State Governments Lobby Washington

Jennifer M. Jensen

Jennifer M. Jensen discusses a lesser-known type of lobbying—that of state and local governments that have lobbying offices in Washington, DC, with the objective of getting money from the federal government. These lobbyists spend a relatively modest amount on lobbying Washington, but the payoff can be significant: federal revenue distributed to the states in 2016 was over $637 billion. These local and state lobbying efforts don't usually show up in lobbying reports, so tracking their activities is difficult. Jensen concludes by saying that when considering lobbying reports, the actions of local and state governments should not be overlooked. Jennifer Jensen is Deputy Provost for Academic Affairs and a professor of political science at Lehigh University. Much of her work examines the relationships between subnational governments and the federal government.

As you read, consider the following questions:

1. How much money is spent a year lobbying Washington, according to the viewpoint?

"Local and state governments lobby the feds much more than you might think," by Jennifer M. Jensen, London School of Economics, March 29, 2019. Reprinted by permission.

2. How much money does the typical local or state government with an office in Washington usually spend?
3. What activities by state and local governments aren't typically considered lobbying?

According to the Center for Responsive Politics, more than 11,000 individual registered lobbyists who actively lobbied the U.S. Congress in 2018. These lobbyists spent more than $3.42 billion making their cases before Congress. While those figures may seem large, they don't even count much of the advocacy by state and local governments.

Lobbyist usually brings to mind someone who represents businesses or trade associations. Or they might represent unions, or membership groups that focus on public interest causes. The National Association of Manufacturers, Google, the United Auto Workers, the American Postal Workers Union, the AARP (formerly American Association of Retired Persons), and the National Rifle Association—each of these is a powerful lobbying organization, and each hires lobbyists to help press their case in Washington.

When they think about lobbyists, most people don't think about the Midwestern Governors Association, a membership organization comprised of the governors of 12 American states. Or the American Association of State Highway and Transportation Officials. Or Miami-Dade County in Florida. Or the Senate of Puerto Rico. Yet each of these organizations has an office in Washington, D.C., that is staffed by professional lobbyists who are either government employees or consultants. State and local government lobbying is a narrow but significant piece of the lobbying ecosystem. Federal revenue distributed to the states in 2016 was over $637 billion, and the federal government also provided funds directly to cities. With that sort of money at stake, the lobbying by subnational governments is significant indeed.

We know less about state and local government lobbying in Washington than we do about other types. Many studies on lobbying in the U.S., including Schlozman and Tierney's seminal 1986 study, have explicitly excluded these types of organizations. Yet a growing number of researchers have focused specifically on state and local government lobbying. For example, monographs by Donald Haider and Anne Marie Camissa have investigated the largest public official associations in Washington. My monograph, *The Governors' Lobbyists*, focuses on political development and activities of the national, regional and partisan governors associations as well as state lobbying offices in Washington; John Nugent has also focused significantly on the National Governors Association (NGA). We have learned how these groups mobilize, and how political context affects them. We have many case studies demonstrating their effectiveness—but it is hard to quantify their effectiveness in dollars returned.

As Frank Baumgartner and Beth Leech point out, it is difficult to determine interest group impact, and that is some of the reason it is difficult to measure just how effective state and local government lobbyists are. But it is also because the most significant players are the associations of public officials, but they typically don't show up in lobbying reports, so it is difficult to track how much they spend.

If the governor of Pennsylvania establishes an office in Washington but hires a consulting firm to work solely for the state, and that consultant lobbies, then that consultant must register as a lobbyist for the state of Pennsylvania, and the state's lobbying activities will appear in the database of congressional lobbying registrations.

But if the governor of Pennsylvania establishes an office in Washington and sends three state employees to work in that office, these employees are not considered lobbyists under the Federal Lobbying Act—even if they gather information, write letters, make calls, and have meetings to advance a political agenda in Congress. They are not lobbyists; they are partners in government. There is no lobbying registration, and no record of lobbying activities. Likewise, public official associations may be organized as a particular legal entity called *instrumentalities of the state* under the U.S. tax code; though they are nonprofit organizations, they do not have to complete I-990 tax forms that provide information on organizational spending. This makes them quite different from nonprofit membership organizations such as the Sierra Club.

None of this activity includes direct advocacy by the public officials who run these governments. If a mayor goes to Washington to meet with her congressional delegation to argue for money for her city, under federal definitions, she isn't lobbying. She is advocating as an arm of the government. But paid lobbyists, often-labeled government relations professionals? The money spent on this sort of lobbying is worth it.

Governments don't spend a lot of money on lobbying. Most state lobbying offices in Washington are comprised of only one or two staff members, and cost a few hundred thousand dollars in salaries, rent and supplies. This is a minuscule part of a state's budget. Even hiring consultants at a relatively expensive hourly rate amounts to chump change. Likewise, cities that engage professional lobbyists are spending tiny amounts of their budgets. And we know that states and localities see rewards from their investments.

So the $3.42 billion in spending by registered lobbyists last year counts private lobbyists, but not the efforts of the public official associations or the full-time state and local government employees who act as lobbyists. The aggregate figure wouldn't change that much if we did include the spending by these groups. Clearly, we have much to learn about the impact of state and local government lobbying—but we know that the impact is there, and we have evidence that at least some types of state and local government lobbying can be extremely financially beneficial for the states and localities paying for lobbyists.

We should remember, when looking at lists of registered lobbyists, that some important and effective players in the lobbying community are being left out.

VIEWPOINT 4

"Many think that the ultimate goal of regulating lobbying is to make lobbying activities transparent. I do not agree. While transparency can be an important value, it has only an instrumental character. The right question here is not how to make lobbying more transparent. Rather, it is how to make public decisions better."

Lobbying Can Make Democracy Work Better

Alberto Bitonti

In this viewpoint, Alberto Bitonti suggests that a new approach to regulating lobbying is necessary. The old approach is to make lobbying more transparent so that the public can view their efforts and where their money goes. Bitonti instead believes that the goal of regulating lobbying should be to improve governmental decision making. Bitonti wants to focus on policymakers and not lobbyists. He believes that this will result in better practical outcomes. Most lobbying regulations, Bitonti believes, are flawed because they rely on the weak assumption that transparency is all that is needed to improve policy making. In light of his suggestions, Bitonti provides his own definition of lobbying regulation, designed to improve how public policy is determined. Alberto Bitonti is a research fellow and lecturer

"How lobbying regulation can make democracy work better," by Alberto Bitonti, European Consortium for Political Research. https://theloop.ecpr.eu/how-lobbying-regulation-can-make-democracy-work-better/. Licensed under CC-BY-ND 4.0 International.

at the Università della Svizzera Italiana. His research is grounded in political philosophy, political science, and communication studies, with a specific research interest in lobbying and public affairs.

As you read, consider the following questions:

1. According to Bitonti, what can political scientists do to improve lobbying regulation?
2. According to Bitonti, what are the "wide variety of measures" besides transparency, that we need to take into consideration when dealing with lobbying?
3. What is Bitonti's definition of lobbying regulation and how does it expand on prevailing thought?

Titus Alexander is right. Political science should aim not only to understand and analyse political dynamics, but also to strengthen democracy and make our lives better.

Lobbying is exactly the kind of area where political scientists may fruitfully bridge scholarly analyses with public discussions and concrete practices. They can better explain the contours of concepts frequently polluted by prejudices and misunderstandings. By doing so, they would help improve the quality of public debates in the media and in the public sphere in general. And, crucially, they can promote sound policy choices.

As political scientists, we can do much in this regard, not least comparing lobbying regulations and analysing why and how they are implemented. We can also reflect on how to fix loopholes, and shed light on the very principles that should guide regulations. In times of democratic malaise, corruption scandals, and crises of representation, rebuilding trust in democratic policymaking—and finding tangible ways to put policymakers in a condition to make better decisions—should be a priority for us all.

Asking the Right Questions

Different political systems around the world continue to devise various types of lobbying regulation. Yet, meanwhile, some questions seem relevant both scientifically and practically.

What is the goal of regulating lobbying? And what are the boundaries of lobbying regulation? My recent *Italian Political Science Review* article with Claudia Mariotti addresses these questions. Our piece highlights the urgent need for a new approach to this matter.

For instance, many think that the ultimate goal of regulating lobbying is to make lobbying activities transparent. I do not agree. While transparency can be an important value, it has only an instrumental character. The right question here is not how to make lobbying more transparent. Rather, it is how to make public decisions better.

In this regard, the prime object of our attention should not be lobbyists, but policymakers. Every lobbying regulation that aspires to be effective should focus not on lobbyists and interest groups, but on policymakers and how they make decisions. This shift in perspective produces relevant practical consequences in terms of principles to pursue.

Fair Access and Policymakers' Accountability

Most reflections in the literature on lobbying regulation focus on the principle of transparency. They study how far different regulatory frameworks shed light on lobbying activities. And most existing lobbying regulations share the same focus. Such regulations aim to make lobbying transparent and easily known to the public, discouraging improper behaviour. As Louis Brandeis famously claimed, "sunlight is said to be the best of disinfectants."

However, other principles are relevant, too, and we should consider them both in regulating lobbying and in studying such regulations. This has been confirmed by practitioners, by the public consultation that the EU Commission made on its Transparency

Register some years ago, as well as by OECD guidelines on this matter. Such principles are:

> *The (fair) equality of access of different interest groups to policymaking processes (for instance, reforming the way consultations and hearings are usually held);*
>
> *the accountability of policymakers themselves (for instance, through the provision of policy footprints and plain-language public communication).*

The philosophies of open government (pursuing more openness) and deliberative democracy (pursuing more deliberative quality) provide solid theoretical arguments to justify such expansion of principles.

That is why most lobbying regulations in the world end up being essentially flawed in the pursuit of their goals. They rely on the weak assumption that transparency is all we need to make things better. But they do not consistently pursue the three principles together. Thus, they generate vast loopholes and insufficiencies.

Regulating Lobbying Is Not Only About Formal Laws

There is another "fix" that political scientists can provide to lobbying regulations (and democracy). It comes from reconsidering the same definition of lobbying regulation. We find lobbying regulation not only in laws on lobbying. Lobbying exceeds the reach of formal laws, as often sub-legislative rules (e.g. internal regulations of ministries and parliaments), norms (habits and customs, codes of conduct, broader political cultures), or even practical frameworks (such as the forms used by governmental authorities for consultations and dialogues with stakeholders, or even the design of digital platforms sometimes used with that purpose) are equally able to "channel" or "steer" the interaction between lobbyists and policymakers in a certain direction.

That is why we cannot look only at transparency registers and enforcement of lobbying laws. Rather, we need to take into consideration a wide variety of other measures, legislative or not. These concern physical access to governmental buildings, political financing, the conflicts of interest of policymakers, the procedures of consultation with stakeholders, the regulatory impact assessments (RIAs) of policies, the more or less institutionalised dialogues between governmental authorities and various interest groups, the legislative/administrative footprints of public decisions, the public agendas of policymakers, and many other aspects that generally affect the interaction between interest groups and policymakers.

That is why we adopt the following definition of lobbying regulation:

> *The set of rules, norms, and frameworks that aim to shape how lobbying is done in a specific political system, regarding a wide range of topics and domains relative to the interaction between policymakers on the one hand and interest groups and lobbyists on the other.*

It follows that there is much to do, even beyond formal legislative processes. Political scientists can thus be leading actors in advocating for reform and engaging with policymakers, on lobbying regulation and other topics, to make democracy work better in concrete ways.

Periodical and Internet Sources Bibliography

The following articles have been selected to supplement the diverse views presented in this chapter.

"Ban Lobbyists from Fundraising for Politicians," the Center for American Progress, April 25, 2018. https://www.americanprogress.org/article/ban-lobbyists-fundraising-politicians/.

"Is Lobbying Good or Bad?" RepresentUS. https://represent.us/action/is-lobbying-good-or-bad/.

Sarah Dickson, "Common Challenges in Lobbying Transparency: Lessons from Europe," Open Government Partnership, June 8, 2021. https://www.opengovpartnership.org/stories/common-challenges-in-lobbying-transparency-lessons-from-europe/.

Taylor Giorno, "Federal lobbying spending tops $1 billion in first quarter of 2023," OpenSecrets, May 1, 2023. https://www.opensecrets.org/news/2023/05/federal-lobbying-spending-tops-1-billion-in-first-quarter-2023/.

Taylor Giorno and Filip Timotija, "Defense sector spent $101 million on lobbying during the first three quarters of 2022," OpenSecrets, November 3, 2022. https://www.opensecrets.org/news/2022/11/defense-sector-spent-101-million-lobbying-during-first-three-quarters-of-2022/.

Ajit Niranjan Glasgow, "Lobbying threat to global climate action," DW, November 5, 2021. https://www.dw.com/en/lobbying-threat-to-global-climate-action/a-59726541.

Karen Nikos-Rose, "Industry Lobbying on WHO Overshadowing Public Health Policy, Researchers Suggest," UC Davis, May 18, 2022. https://www.ucdavis.edu/news/industry-lobbying-who-overshadowing-public-health-policy-researchers-suggest.

Rebecca Pifer, "Healthcare lobbying rose 70% over past two decades," Healthcare Dive, October 31, 2022. https://www.healthcaredive.com/news/healthcare-lobbying-expenditures-phrma-hospital/635337/.

Stephen Semler, "How the Military-Industrial Complex Gets Its Power and Harms Workers, in 6 Graphs," *Jacobin*, October 13,

2022. https://jacobin.com/2022/10/pentagon-budget-military-contractors-lobbyists-biden.

Edward Segal, "How and Why Corporate Lobbying Will Continue to Matter During The Biden Administration," *Forbes*, January 26, 2021. https://www.forbes.com/sites/edwardsegal/2021/01/26/how-and-why-corporate-lobbying-will-continue-to-matter-during-the-biden-administration/?sh=3971e98144dd.

Rory Sullivan, Robert Black, and Georgina Kyriacou, "What is climate change lobbying?," The London School of Economics and Political Science, February 17, 2023. https://www.lse.ac.uk/granthaminstitute/explainers/what-is-climate-change-lobbying/.

Peter Ubel, Why Is Healthcare So Expensive? Blame The Lobbyists. *Forbes*, April 9, 2021. https://www.forbes.com/sites/peterubel/2021/04/09/why-is-healthcare-so-expensive-blame-the-lobbyists/.

Philip A. Wallach, "America's lobbying addiction," Brookings Institution, April 13, 2015. https://www.brookings.edu/blog/fixgov/2015/04/13/americas-lobbying-addiction/.

Daniel Weiser, "Why Lobbying Is Legal and Important in the U.S." *Investopedia*, September 28, 2023. https://www.investopedia.com/articles/investing/043015/why-lobbying-legal-and-important-us.asp.

For Further Discussion

Chapter 1

1. After reading the viewpoints in this chapter, do you think the *Citizens United* decision by the Supreme Court was a positive or negative development? Explain your answer.
2. Do you think that the *Citizens United* decision should be overturned? Why or why not?
3. After reading the viewpoint by Lyon on the effects of *Citizens United* in the present day, how do you think it will continue to affect U.S. politics going forward?

Chapter 2

1. After reading the viewpoints in this chapter, do you think politicians are less ethical now than in the past? Why or why not?
2. After reading the viewpoints in this chapter, do you think elected legislators should be able to trade stocks? Why or why not?
3. After reading the viewpoint by McClure, do you think judges should be allowed to accept campaign donations? Do you think the law that says they cannot accept money directly is fair? Explain your reasoning.

Chapter 3

1. After reading the viewpoints in this chapter, do you think that lying or stretching the truth is an essential aspect of politics? Explain your answer.
2. Do you believe that politicians should be punished for lying to the public? Why or why not?
3. After reading the viewpoint by Bufacchi, do you think that former President Trump is more deceitful than previous presidents? Explain your answer.

Chapter 4

1. After reading the viewpoints in this chapter, do you believe that lobbying encourages unethical behavior by politicians? Explain your answer.
2. After reading the viewpoints in this chapter, do you think that lobbying creates an uneven playing field for the wealthy and powerful? Why or why not?
3. After reading the viewpoint by Bitonti, do you agree or disagree that lobbying can improve a democratic society? Explain your answer.

Organizations to Contact

The editors have compiled the following list of organizations concerned with the issues debated in this book. The descriptions are derived from materials provided by the organizations. All have publications or information available for interested readers. The list was compiled on the date of publication of the present volume; the information provided here may change. Be aware that many organizations take several weeks or longer to respond to inquiries, so allow as much time as possible.

American Enterprise Institute for Public Policy Research (AEI)

American Enterprise Institute
1789 Massachusetts Avenue, NW
Washington, DC 20036
(202) 862-5800
email: tyler.castle@aei.org
website: www.aei.org

The American Enterprise Institute is a conservative public policy think tank that sponsors original research on the world economy, U.S. foreign policy and international security, and domestic political and social issues. AEI is dedicated to defending human dignity, expanding human potential, and building a freer and safer world. Their scholars and staff advance ideas rooted in their belief in democracy and free enterprise.

The Bipartisan Policy Center (BPC)

1225 Eye Street, NW Suite 1000
Washington, DC 20005
(202) 204-2400
email: bipartisaninfo@bipartisanpolicy.org
website: www.bipartisanpolicy.org

The Bipartisan Policy Center is a Washington, DC-based think tank that actively fosters bipartisanship by combining the best ideas from both parties to promote health, security, and opportunity for all Americans. Its policy solutions are the product of informed deliberations by former elected and appointed officials, business and labor leaders, and academics and advocates who represent both sides of the political spectrum. According to its website, BPC prioritizes one thing above all else: getting things done.

The Brookings Institution

1775 Massachusetts Ave., NW
Washington, DC 20036
(202) 797-6000
email: communications@brookings.edu
website: www.brookings.edu

The Brookings Institution is a non-profit public policy organization based in Washington, DC. Its mission is to conduct in-depth research that leads to new ideas for solving problems facing society at the local, national, and global level. Brookings brings together more than 300 leading experts in government and academia from all over the world who provide research, policy recommendations, and analysis on a full range of public policy issues. Its research agenda and recommendations are rooted in open-minded inquiry and represent diverse points of view. Research topics cover foreign policy, economics, development, governance, and metropolitan policy.

Cato Institute

1000 Massachusetts Avenue NW
Washington, DC 20001
(202) 842-0200
website: www.cato.org

The Cato Institute is a libertarian public policy research organization and think tank dedicated to the principles of individual liberty, limited government, free markets, and peace. Its scholars and analysts conduct independent research on a wide range of policy issues.

Center for American Progress

1333 H Street NW, Suite 100E
Washington, DC 20005
(202) 682-1611
website: www.americanprogress.org

The Center for American Progress is a public policy research and advocacy organization which presents a liberal viewpoint on economic and social issues. Its website contains reports on topics such as democracy and government; and politics and elections.

David Horowitz Freedom Center

PO Box 55089
Sherman Oaks, CA 91499
(800) 752-6562
website: www.horowitzfreedomcenter.org

Founded in 1988 by political activist David Horowitz and Peter Collier, the David Horowitz Freedom Center (formerly the Center for the Study of Popular Culture) was established with funding from conservative groups. It runs several websites and blogs, including *FrontPage Magazine*, Students for Academic Freedom, and Jihad Watch.

Freedom House

1850 M Street NW, 11th Floor
Washington, DC 20036
(202) 296-5101
email: info@freedomhouse.org
website: http://freedomhouse.org

Freedom House advocates for a U.S. foreign policy that places the promotion of democracy as a priority. Its representatives regularly testify before Congress, provide briefings to high level administration and State Department officials, and argue the case for freedom at conferences, in op-eds, and through media appearances. Freedom House serves as a leading advocate for policies to advance worldwide democracy. Its website contains numerous relevant materials, including a section on "Election Integrity."

The Heritage Foundation

214 Massachusetts Ave NE
Washington DC 20002
(800) 546-2843
email: info@heritage.org
website: www.heritage.org

The Heritage Foundation is a conservative think tank. The organization's mission is to formulate and promote conservative public policies based on the principles of free enterprise, limited government, individual freedom, traditional American values, and a strong national defense.

Mises Institute

518 West Magnolia Avenue
Auburn, Alabama 36832
(334) 321-2100
website: www.mises.org

Mises Institute is a libertarian think tank in researching and promoting viewpoints about subjects such as economics, philosophy, and political economy. Named for the famous Austrian School economist, the Institute's stated mission is to promote "the Misesian tradition of thought through the defense of the market economy, private property, sound money, and peaceful international relations, while opposing government intervention."

National Endowment for Democracy (NED)

1201 Pennsylvania Ave, NW, Suite 1100
Washington, DC 20004
(202) 378-9700
email: info@NED.org
website: www.ned.org

Founded in 1983, the National Endowment for Democracy (NED) is a private, non-profit foundation dedicated to the growth and strengthening of democratic institutions around the world. NED is dedicated to fostering the growth of a wide range of democratic institutions abroad, including political parties, trade unions, free markets, and business organizations, as well as the many elements of a vibrant civil society that ensure human rights, an independent media, and the rule of law.

The Progressive Policy Institute (PPI)

1156 15th Street NW, Suite 400
Washington, DC 20005
Phone: (202) 525-3926
email: info@ppionline.org
website: www.progressivepolicy.org

The Progressive Policy Institute is a catalyst for policy innovation and political reform based in Washington, DC. Its mission is to create radically pragmatic ideas for moving America beyond ideological and partisan deadlock. Founded in 1989, PPI started as the intellectual home of the New Democrats and earned a reputation as President Bill Clinton's "idea mill." Many of its mold-breaking ideas have been translated into public policy and law and have influenced international efforts to modernize progressive politics.

Bibliography of Books

Gregg Barak. *Criminology on Trump*. London, UK: Routledge, 2022.

Emanuela Ceva and Maria Paola Ferretti. *Political Corruption: The Internal Enemy of Public Institutions*. New York, NY: Oxford University Press, 2021.

Anthony M. Clohesy. *The Politics of Well-Being: Toward a More Ethical World*. New York: Routledge, 2021.

Roger D. Congleton. *Solving Social Dilemmas: Ethics, Politics, and Prosperity*. New York, NY: Oxford University Press, 2022.

Nicole M. Elias and Amanda M. Olejarski, eds. *Ethics for Contemporary Bureaucrats: Navigating Constitutional Crossroads*. New York, NY: Routledge, 2020.

Bob Fischer. *Ethics, Left and Right: The Moral Issues that Divide Us*. New York, NY: Oxford University Press, 2020.

Edward Hall and Andrew Sabl. *Political Ethics: A Handbook*. Princeton, NJ: Princeton University Press, 2022.

Annabelle Lever and Andrei Poama, eds. *The Routledge Handbook of Ethics and Public Policy*. Abingdon, UK: Routledge, 2020.

Catriona McKinnon. *Climate Change and Political Theory*. Cambridge, UK: Polity Press, 2022.

Edward U. Murphy. *The Politics of Compassion: The Challenge to Care for the Stranger*. London, UK: Rowman & Littlefield, 2019.

Reinhold Niebuhr. *Moral Man and Immoral Society a Study in Ethics and Politics*. Victoria, BC: Must Have Books, 2021.

Robert North Roberts. *The Death of Public Integrity*. New York, NY: Routledge, 2020.

Joseph S. Nye. *Do Morals Matter?: Presidents and Foreign Policy from FDR to Trump*. New York, NY: Oxford University Press, 2020.

Jonathan Sacks. *Morality: Restoring the Common Good in Divided Times*. London, UK: Hodder & Stoughton, 2020.

Theresa Scavenius. *Political Responsibility for Climate Change: Ethical Institutions and Fact-Sensitive Theory*. Abingdon, UK: Routledge, 2020.

Audrey Wells. *Rule Of Reverse Results: The Effects of Unethical Policies*? Abingdon, UK: Routledge, 2021.

Index

E

F

G

I

J

K

L

M

N

O

P

R

S

T

U

V

W